GROW UP, TAHLIA WILKINS!

GROW UP, TAHLIA WILKINS!

KARINA EVANS

LB
LITTLE, BROWN AND COMPANY
New York Boston

This book is a work of fiction. Names, characters, places, and incidents are the product of the author's imagination or are used fictitiously. Any resemblance to actual events, locales, or persons, living or dead, is coincidental.

Little, Brown and Company
Hachette Book Group
1290 Avenue of the Americas, New York, NY 10104
Visit us at LBYR.com

First Edition: April 2022

Little, Brown and Company is a division of Hachette Book Group, Inc. The Little, Brown name and logo are trademarks of Hachette Book Group, Inc.

The publisher is not responsible for websites (or their content) that are not owned by the publisher.

Library of Congress Cataloging-in-Publication Data
Names: Evans, Karina, author.
Title: Grow up, Tahlia Wilkins! / Karina Evans.
Description: First edition. | New York : Little, Brown and Company, 2022. | Audience: Ages 8–12. | Summary: "Twelve-year-old Tahlia Wilkins has to deal with getting her first period just before the biggest pool party of the year." —Provided by publisher.
Identifiers: LCCN 2020053392 | ISBN 9780316168755 (hardcover) | ISBN 9780316168922 (ebook) | ISBN 9780316168656 (ebook other)
Subjects: CYAC: Puberty—Fiction. | Menstruation—Fiction. | Best friends—Fiction. | Friendship—Fiction. | Family life—Fiction. | Popularity—Fiction.
Classification: LCC PZ7.1.E8696 Gro 2022 | DDC [Fic]—dc23
LC record available at https://lccn.loc.gov/2020053392

ISBNs: 978-0-316-16875-5 (hardcover), 978-0-316-16892-2 (ebook)

Printed in the United States of America

LSC-C

Printing 1, 2022

To those who are going through big changes, learning more about their bodies, and figuring out what defines them

CHAPTER ONE

It's official—my traitorous chin is growing a zit.

Well, I guess I'm not *exactly* positive—I could probably count on one hand the number of pimples I've had—but I'm pretty sure the throbbing feeling just below my lower lip did not come from some bee that managed to fly into Mrs. Brown's classroom and sting my face without anyone noticing.

The timing could not be worse. I do not want to have a pimple right in time for the most important event of my life—Noah Campos's pool party.

A.k.a. the event that will make or break my entire summer.

Since Noah is the most popular kid in the seventh grade, the pool party is all anyone's been talking about for the last month of school. Anyone who has been invited, that is. Pretty sure Alexa Arnecki, the girl who still brings dolls to school, and Keith Green, the kid who wears pajama pants to class and serenades people on their birthday, won't be there.

It's my chance to prove to everyone that I am *not* the same girl who wore a one-piece bathing suit with knee-length board shorts and goggles to Noah's start-of-summer pool party last year. No sirree!

I cringe at the memory. I'd worn the board shorts so that my legs wouldn't get burned in the sun, and I'd worn the goggles because I thought we'd be doing flips into the pool and I didn't want to get water in my eyes. But when I got there, all the other girls were in cute bathing suits. Even Hannah Bean, who'd worn oversized soccer jerseys to school every single day last year, had on a fun two-piece suit for the party.

How was I the only one to miss the memo? Hadn't we all just learned in Mr. Richard's sixth-grade class how important it was to cover up to prevent too much sun exposure?

Everyone had laughed at me and asked if I was planning on going tide-pooling. I even heard them whispering about my "baby goggles" for the rest of the party.

I cannot let that happen to me again.

But now, my throbbing chin threatens to ruin everything. What if a whole zit cluster pops up? A pack of pimples does not scream *new and improved*. It screams, *Look at these planets on my face!* And it's just my luck. Now I have less than twenty-four hours before the party to destroy my soon-to-be pimple solar system. *Greeaat.*

I run my finger over the throbbing area before swiping open the front-facing camera on my phone to stare at my chin. The camera angle makes my face look like a thumb.

Yup, it's a growing pimple, all right. A biggie too. And it gets redder and redder the more I poke at it, trying to force it to go back down.

Am I supposed to know how to get rid of this bulging life-ruiner? I've never seen Noah Campos poking around on *his* face. Maybe he knows of some secret anti-acne formula.

"Ahem. Tahlia?"

I look up to see my teacher, Mrs. Brown, staring at me from the front of the classroom with her arms crossed.

I gulp. I'd almost forgotten I was still in class.

"I know it's the last day of school, but I still need your attention until the bell rings, yes?" She raises an eyebrow. "No phones."

I quickly set my phone screen-down on my desk and give her my best "I'm genuinely sorry" expression.

Mrs. Brown nods and continues on with whatever she was saying.

I look over my shoulder to see my best friend, Lily, rolling her eyes. Lily's dark hair is pulled up into a bun, and her purple braces match her purple-striped shirt. I think the purple-on-purple combo makes her seem even younger than she is. She's already the youngest in our grade, so the bright colors make her look like a little crayon. Sometimes I wish she'd outgrow all the matchy-matchy, but I'd never tell her that.

Lily and I met on the very first day of kindergarten, and we've been practically sisters ever since, so she knows me well enough to see I'm definitely *not* sorry for ignoring Mrs. Brown. And why should I be? We took our end-of-the-year tests two weeks ago, and we haven't learned anything since. My pimple emergency is much more important than listening to Mrs. Brown go on about how much of a "pleasure" it's been to have us in her class. Teachers have to say stuff like that, even if they don't mean it—and in this case, Mrs. Brown definitely doesn't. I personally saw Amir Abdi jam a pencil up his nose and try to take a pop quiz without using his hands. Twice. That was not a "pleasure" to watch.

"And that's why I know you'll all do great next year on the eighth-grade side of campus," finishes Mrs. Brown. "It's been so nice getting to know you all."

From her seat behind Lily, Jackie Berg raises

her hand and starts talking before Mrs. Brown has a chance to call on her.

"When do we get our class schedules for next year?" Jackie asks, flipping her long hair behind her shoulder.

Jackie used to hang out with Lily and me every weekend in elementary school—in fact, when we started classes this year, she even rode her bike to school with us. But ever since she started straightening her hair and wearing shoes not meant for pedaling, she stopped biking and started having her parents drop her off. Now she spends the weekends with popular kids like Noah Campos.

I tried asking my parents to drive Lily and me to school, but they laughed me out of the room. So I'm doomed to helmet hair and dirty sneakers.

"Sometime in August," Mrs. Brown answers.

I pick at my chin. I think I read somewhere that yogurt is good to smear on pimples. Or was it mayonnaise? I can't remember now. Ugh! School just needs to be over so I can figure this out.

"Anyway"—Mrs. Brown looks up at the clock

on the wall—"I know the last bell is about to ring and you'll go racing out of here, but enjoy your summer and make sure to come visit me and the rest of your seventh-grade teachers next year!" She claps her hands together with a big grin.

On cue, the last bell finally goes off, and a few kids throw their papers up in the air and let them flutter to the floor. I grab my phone and swipe open the camera again to look at my chin as the rest of the class gathers their things and hustles out of the room.

"Leave it alone!" Lily whispers as she comes up behind me.

The very fact that she knows what I'm picking at means that she can see the growing zit, which does *not* make me want to leave it alone. It makes me want to pick at it until it's completely gone.

"Easy for you to say. *You've* never had one." I frown.

Lily rolls her eyes. "Come on," she says, tugging my arm and pulling me out of my desk. "My mom wants me to come straight home after school."

I sigh and stand. We really can't dawdle if Lily's mom wants her home. Her mom is eight months' pregnant, so whatever she says goes.

Yup, that's right—pregnant. As in, with a real live baby. I nearly choked on a pretzel when Lily told me the news. My best friend being a big sister? It's just so weird. And unexpected. But I've accepted it now.

Mostly.

Lily and I march out of the classroom and head toward the bike rack. A group of eighth graders are celebrating finishing middle school by taking pictures in front of our school's sign. They laugh and pose as they take turns snapping the photos, making sure all their friends have a chance to be in a big group shot. It looks fun.

If Noah's party goes well tomorrow, maybe when Lily and I graduate middle school next year, it won't be just the two of us taking pictures of each other. We might even have our *own* group. Sigh.

When we reach our bikes, Jackie is leaning up against the rack and scrolling through her phone.

"Hey, Jackie!" Lily waves.

I try not to groan. Lily is always so nice to her. It's like she doesn't even care that Jackie used to be our close friend before she ditched us. She *used* to be part of our little group. One day we were all eating lunch together, and the next Jackie was across the cafeteria, laughing with her new friends. We hadn't even been in a fight or anything. She just... left.

Jackie glances up from her phone. "Oh, hey, guys." She looks back down at the screen and keeps scrolling.

"Are you going to Noah's pool party tomorrow?" Lily asks excitedly.

Tomorrow will be Lily's first time going to one of Noah's parties. She had a stomach bug last year, so she wasn't there to witness my horrible goggles-and-board-shorts incident. She only heard about it later.

I know I really can't blame Lily for being sick, but sometimes I can't help but think that if she *had* been there, then at least there would have been two of us who didn't get the cute-suit alert. And I know for a fact that Lily would've worn her purple rash-guard, because she doesn't like when her shoulders peel after being in the sun too long.

Jackie nods. "Mhmm, are you?"

"Yup!" Lily beams. "We're going to ride over to Noah's from Tahlia's house."

"You're biking?" Jackie looks at us as if we've just told her we step in dog poop for fun.

"No," I say quickly, even though we *were* planning to take our bikes. "Riding—as in a car." It's the only thing I can think to say to make her stop looking at us with a raised eyebrow.

"Okay," Jackie says, smiling. "Cool. And no board shorts and baby goggles this year, right, Tahlia?" She smirks.

My stomach sinks.

Jackie was still our friend last summer. She knows how embarrassing the party was for me, because I *specifically* told her. She even helped me pick out my first two-piece bathing suit afterward so that it would never happen again. I *hate* that Jackie has all this secret knowledge about stuff I told her when we could trust her, and now she just uses it to remind me she doesn't hang out with me anymore.

I know it bothers Lily too, but Lily is always so friendly to her. It's annoying. I wish she would dislike Jackie like I do, but instead Lily acts extra nice to her, as if she thinks it'll somehow convince Jackie we're still fun to hang out with. Yeah, right. Like that'll ever work.

There's a car honk from behind us.

"That's my mom," Jackie says as she slings her backpack over her shoulder. "But I'll see you tomorrow, sevies!" She gives us a wave before racing over to the pickup loop, where her mom's car is waiting.

I frown at her use of *sevies*. It's what the eighth graders used to call us seventh graders, and it never felt like a compliment. Besides, her saying it doesn't even make any sense. She's in the same grade we are. We're all technically now *eighties*.

Lily doesn't seem to mind the term, because she turns to me and asks, "What's wrong with biking?"

"Nothing," I say, but it comes out a bit ruder than I mean it, so I add, "I don't know." Which is the truth—I honestly don't. Biking is fun and useful. I have no idea when and why it became uncool.

Lily shrugs. "Me neither."

She clips on her helmet, pulls her bike out from the rack, and swings her leg over it. I follow her lead.

"Ready?" Lily asks.

I nod.

We take off toward our neighborhood, passing the line of parents waiting to pick up their kids from school. I wonder which car is Noah's. I've never seen *him* bike to school.

Lily leads us onto the next street and picks up her pace. She loves to go fast. Usually, I do too, but today, even though I know I should be happy that school has ended and summer is starting, I can't help getting a little bit grumpier with every rotation of my pedals.

But tomorrow's party will be my chance to make everything right. I'll wear my new two-piece bathing suit with *no* board shorts and *no* baby goggles. That way, even Jackie won't have anything to poke fun at me for.

As long as the pool party goes according to my plan, and I can get rid of the pimple on my chin in time, then everything will be fine. I just can't spend another summer as some big joke. I'll show everyone that I am new and improved.

I let out a deep breath and tighten my grip on the bike.

Everything will be better after the pool party. It *has* to be.

CHAPTER TWO

When we reach the street where Lily turns left toward her house and I turn right toward mine, Lily bikes up onto the sidewalk and comes to a stop. I pull up beside her.

"Last ride of the year," she says and smiles.

"Just think, next time we're here, we'll be *eighth* graders." Even though I'm still a little grumpy, the thought of being one of the oldest kids at school sends a bit of giddy excitement through me.

But Lily doesn't answer. She looks down and

brushes dirt off her pants. I bet she's picturing starting the new school year with a new baby sibling at home.

"I'll text you in the morning about going to Noah's together," I say.

"Hopefully, that thing on your chin will be gone by then," she says, chuckling.

I gasp. "Lily!"

She laughs and picks her foot off the ground to pedal forward.

"See you tomorrow!" she calls over her shoulder. "*Eighth* grader!"

I stick my tongue out at her but immediately realize it's not something the new and improved Tahlia would do, so I suck it back in before anyone can see.

When Lily has biked around the corner, I push off the ground and start home. Three streets later, I walk my bike up my driveway before dropping it in the grass. I know Mom will want me to bring it around to the backyard, but that's a chore for another time.

"There's our seventh-grade graduate!" Mom says when I step through the front door. "How was your last day of school?"

Mom is wearing one of her professional work outfits and frantically stuffing things into her purse. The tips of her hair are damp from a shower, and they've made small wet marks on the shoulders of her blouse. It's a common look for her. She's always rushing out of the shower to get places. I must've inherited the being-on-time trait from Dad—definitely not from her.

"Good," I say, shrugging. I don't have time to chitchat. I need to get yogurt. Or mayonnaise. Or maybe both. Yeah, both. I'll smear them both on my chin.

"Great!" She smiles. Then she motions to a stack of boxes near the door that leads out to the garage. "I know you just got home, but can you help me carry these to the car?"

"Where are Jamie and Ryan?" I ask. Usually, my twin sixteen-year-old brothers spend their afternoons playing video games while lounging on the couch. How suspiciously *convenient* that they just so happen to be missing when the chores get dished out.

"Can you please just help bring these out? I'm running late as it is," she says as she picks up a box and shuffles into the garage.

"Whoa, Tahlia, did you hurt your chin?" Dad asks as he walks into the living room from the garage. He points at my face before bending down to pick up a box.

"Da-ad!" I slap a hand over my zit. If my dad—a man who didn't even notice when Mom accidentally dyed her hair purple after using one of those do-it-yourself dye kits—can notice my growing chin pimple, I've really got a serious problem.

There's no time to waste. I need to deal with it *immediately* if there's any chance of it being gone by Noah's party.

"I'll be right back!" I exclaim as I turn on my heel.

Before I can sprint into the kitchen for yogurt, Dad says, "Wait, wait, wait! You can help your mom first for five seconds."

"But—!"

Dad gives me one of his "Don't even try it" looks.

I exhale loudly. "Fine," I say as I march toward the boxes. "What's in these things anyway?" I bend down to lift one of them up. It's heavy.

"Stuff for my work retreat," Mom answers as she walks back into the room. "Team-building games and snacks, mostly." She picks up a box and hauls it toward the garage.

I eye the box in my arms. "What kind of snacks?"

"Please just bring it to the car, Tahlia," she calls over her shoulder.

"Yeah, yeah," I mumble.

One of the many *joys* of Mom running her own small business is that we always get roped in to help her do the grunt work. Cue eye roll.

Although, in the case of *this* grunt work, the sooner I get it done, the sooner Mom will hit the road. And with her gone, I can get my chin ready for Noah's party in peace. So I hurry to load the box in the trunk.

When I trudge back into the living room, Dad

passes by me carrying the last box to the car. Mom sneaks up behind me and plants a kiss on my head. I grimace, and she pulls me into a hug.

"I shouldn't have scheduled the work retreat for this weekend." She frowns. "I wish we all could've had a big dinner tonight to celebrate you kids' last day of school. We'll do something later."

"Yup, got it. Have fun at your work thingy," I say, wiggling free of the hug.

"And you have fun at the pool party tomorrow," she says while pulling on a jacket. "I think I saw your board shorts in your closet."

I make a face. "Urgh, no. I'm not wearing *those*."

Mom raises an eyebrow. "Okay, well, remember to reapply sunscreen after swimming."

"I will," I grumble. "Oh, and I need a ride to the party."

"Why can't you bike?"

I ignore the question and whine, "Mom, *please*?"

She's distracted and fumbling with her keys as she says, "Ask your dad. He's the one who will need to take you over."

On cue, Dad walks back into the house. I turn to face him.

"Dad," I say sweetly, "can you drive me over to Noah's pool party tomorrow?"

"Uh, sure," he grunts as he lifts Mom's suitcase and brings it into the garage.

I grin.

"I'll be back tomorrow night. Late, probably," Mom says. "And remember, on Monday we're meeting with the school counselor to go over the various elective options for next year."

Ugh.

I make a face and try not to groan aloud. While I *am* excited to be the oldest at school next year, the very last thing I want to think about right now is actually taking eighth-grade classes. I literally just finished seventh grade *today*! Can't a girl get a little relax time? Sheesh!

Mom notices my annoyed expression. "It's always good to be prepared, Tahlia. Summer goes faster than you think. And maybe if you look into taking some new extracurricular activities, you'll make more friends!"

She's made comments like this ever since Jackie stopped hanging out with Lily and me. Honestly, I think she was more upset about it than I was. I couldn't care less that Jackie thinks she is too cool for us now. Not one bit. Nada. Why would *I* want to be friends with someone who doesn't want to be friends with me? I don't!

I mean, yeah, maybe a *few* more not-Jackie friends would be nice, but I'm not about to tell Mom that. She'd do something embarrassing like try to set up a "playdate" for me with one of her work friends' kids, who are all younger than I am. No, thank you!

Besides, after tomorrow, I won't even need Mom's help. If I can prove to Noah that I'm cooler than I was last year, then maybe everyone else in my grade will think so too. Then it won't matter at all what *Jackie* thinks.

I'm about to answer Mom, when the twins walk into the living room from the door that leads to our backyard. They're sweaty and gross. They must have some sort of telepathic way of knowing when chores are finished. I'd envy them if they weren't so disgusting.

"There you two are." Mom smiles at them. "Come here. Come give me a hug before I take off."

"What incredible timing you two have," I say sarcastically to the twins as they walk over to hug Mom goodbye.

They smirk at me. I glare back.

Most people have trouble figuring out which twin is which, but it's easy for me. Jamie looks like a doofus because his ears are too big, and Ryan looks like a doofus because his neck is too long. See? Easy.

"All right, I'm off." Mom slings her purse over her shoulder and gives Dad a kiss. "You can call me for the next hour if you need anything. But remember, I won't have service once I'm at the work retreat, since it's in Forest County."

"Bye, Mom," I say.

"Bye, Mom," Jamie and Ryan echo as they plop themselves down on the couch.

"See you guys tomorrow night. And congrats again on finishing the school year—yay!" Mom blows us kisses before hustling into the garage.

A few moments later, I hear the automatic garage door slowly open and the car rumble to a start.

Dad sits next to my brothers on the couch, and Ryan (the one with the long neck) reaches for the remote to switch on the TV.

"Tahlia," Jamie (the one with the large ears) says, pointing to my chin, "you've got a little something-something happening on your face. It's not a good 'something.' "

My eyes widen in horror. I'd almost forgotten about my rapidly expanding chin bump!

Without a second thought, I race into our downstairs guest bathroom. As soon as I close the door behind me, I hear Jamie and Ryan snicker from the couch.

Oh, what I'd give for a cool older sister instead of brainless brothers. Sigh.

I squint into the mirror and get to work on destroying the UFO (unwanted face object). But after ten minutes of poking, prodding, and squeezing, all I manage to do is create a little sweat line across my brow from concentrating so hard. The chin zit will *not* be easily removed. I think it must sense fear.

I'm about to give up, slap a Band-Aid across my face, and claim I was in some freak chin-only accident (maybe I'll also get sympathy points), when there's a strange feeling in my *nether regions*—you know, the area *down below.*

Confused, I undo my pants, sit down on the toilet, look down...

And—

Holy Mother of Aunt Josephine. *It* has finally happened.

Wait—has it? I'm not sure. I'm not sure what *it* is meant to look like.

I squint a little closer. No, no, it has *absolutely* happened.

The Fairy Godmother of Puberty has paid me my first visit.

Translation? I, Tahlia Wilkins, have started my period in our tiny downstairs bathroom.

CHAPTER THREE

Oh.

My.

God.

This can't be happening. Not now.

When I said "new and improved," this is NOT what I meant. I knew it would happen eventually, of course. I mean, it's already happened to most of the girls in my grade. I just never thought it would happen *today*.

I should be excited.

I *am* excited.

Aren't I excited?

Okay, I guess I'm *somewhat* excited but mostly freaking out.

Don't get me wrong, I do know the basics of how it all works, thanks to Mrs. Brown's super awkward health class. And Jackie wouldn't shut up about it to Lily and me when it happened to her last year.

The only thing is, Mom was supposed to take me to the store before the new monthly gift arrived. That way I'd be prepared. That way I wouldn't be in the very situation I'm in right now!

Why, oh why, didn't she take me to the store!?

Well, fine. I do know why.

It's because she tried to take me while Dad was in the car. So naturally, I had to pretend that I had a bunch of homework to finish and we didn't have time to stop. I was not about to go into the *menstrual products* aisle with Dad around. My dad is the most awkward person on planet Earth!

Last year, after Mom and I went bra shopping, we met up with Dad and the twins for dinner, and I made the mistake of bringing my new bag of purchases into the restaurant with me. When Dad saw the bag, he asked if I was happy with my new bra purchase loudly enough for everyone inside to hear! What the heck am I supposed to say to that with everyone listening?

Um, yeah, Dad. I'm super happy with my new boob holder, thanks for asking!

I've never been so mortified in my entire life.

So, obviously, there was no way I was going period-product shopping with him. Mom should have known to take me back later *alone*.

And now, of course, just as luck would have it, she's left on her work retreat, so I can't even shout for her to come help me in the bathroom. Plus, I've thoughtlessly left my phone in my backpack by the front door, so I can't quickly call her from the bathroom to demand she stop driving and turn around to come home this instant.

Super excellent timing, Mom.

Not!

I sigh and look down between my feet at the only evidence of my period's arrival—my ruined underwear. I stare at them as I think of what to do next.

It's not like I can just pull the underwear back up as if nothing is there. If I do that, the stain will definitely go through to my jeans, and there's no way I am going to ruin the only jeans that manage to give me some semblance of curves. Before I started wearing these jeans, Jackie used to call me a "walking string bean."

But it's not like I can just take the underwear off either. That would mean leaving them in this tiny bathroom for everyone to see—or, worse, walking out into the living room with them in my hand.

If I were in the upstairs bathroom, then *maybe* I'd be able to quickly run across the hall with them without anyone seeing, but in this bathroom, there is slim chance of that. This bathroom is only a few feet from where Jamie, Ryan, and Dad are watching TV. It's far too likely that they'll see me carrying the evidence.

Oh, how naive I was just ten minutes ago when I waltzed into this bathroom thinking my chin pimple was the only thing trying to ruin my life before Noah's party.

Ah, the good ol' days.

I sigh and look back down at the red mark. It's still there. I think it might be getting bigger.

Holy Mother of Uncle Harold!

Mom really hates it when I use that "Holy Mother of" phrase. She thinks it's weird, since we aren't religious and I just make up the names. The only person who gets it is Lily.

Whenever I exclaim, "Holy Mother of Aunt Blah-Blah-Blah," Lily always nods and says, "You've got that right," as if it makes the most sense in the world. Lily *always* understands me. She gets me way more than Jackie ever did.

I groan.

If only Mom hadn't just left on her annoying work retreat. Now that she's gone, I'm stuck with the menfolk of the family, and I have no desire whatsoever to inform them of my current situation. I would rather drink a gallon of chunky milk than admit to Dad—king of awkward—that the Red Goddess of Panties has arrived in my underwear.

And if Jamie or Ryan found out? Please plan my funeral now for when I die of embarrassment.

What's worse than having your brothers know you're *menstruating*?

So, no, that's not happening. I need to think of something else.

Which brings me back to staring down at the stain between my feet and figuring out what in the world I'm going to do.

What I need is a sanitary napkin.

Now there's a term I don't like—*sanitary napkin*. It makes me think of Mrs. Brown at the front of the class holding up a large, diaper-looking cotton pad and explaining all the technical aspects of a woman's *ovaries* and *tubes*.

I choke down a nervous laugh. *Tubes*. I think I'm losing it. Why am I laughing at a time like this?

I also don't like the term *menstruation products*. Can't explain why. It just makes me cringe. Maybe it's because it sounds like something my grandma Judy would say.

Well, whatever I decide to call it, I need one. Right now.

I check the small cabinet under the bathroom sink to see if Mom stuffed some products in there, but no such luck. All that's under there are old cleaning supplies, and I really don't think antibacterial shower spray is going to help me right now.

I let out a small whimper.

There's a knock on the bathroom door, and I freeze.

"Tahlia?" Dad's voice is muffled by the door. "You okay in there?"

"I'm fine!" I say back a bit too quickly.

I can hear Jamie and Ryan chuckle from the couch, again. They probably think I'm stinking the place up since I've now been in here for more than fifteen minutes.

"You sure?" Dad asks.

"Obviously!" I squeak out through nervous laughter. I need to make it seem like *he's* the crazy one.

Duh, Dad. All twelve-year-olds take this long to go to the bathroom. Didn't you know?

"All right," Dad responds, and I hear his footsteps walking away from the door.

I really need to get out of here. If I spend any more time in this bathroom staring at my underwear, Dad will go to the store and buy me antidiarrheals.

I take a deep breath, close my eyes, and come up with a plan.

First item in my plan—I need to call Mom. This instant.

The longer I wait to call her, the less chance there is that she'll turn around and help me. But before I can call her, I need to figure out how to leave this bathroom without ruining my jeans.

Something Jackie once blabbed pops into my mind. She told us that when her first period arrived, she had to stuff her underwear with toilet paper because she was at school without any pads.

I look over at the toilet paper roll next to the flowery-smelling candle my parents bought at a craft market. The paper hangs limply. The thought of shoving the itchy stuff into my pants is not remotely enticing.

But with no other options, I groan, roll out a long piece of toilet paper, fold it into a little rectangle, and place it in my underwear over the stain. Then I pull the underwear back up, zip my pants, and give my hands an extra-thorough wash. As I run my hands under the water, I look at myself in the mirror.

Do I look like a woman now?

Answer: Definitely not.

I think my pink-and-blue braces shut down any chance of *that* happening. Plus, my unbrushed, curly hair sticks out in every direction, my nose is still peeling from last week's sunburn, and the giant zit has gained total control of the lower half of my face. Yeah, you could say I'm a total cutie.

A twelve-year-old babe with folded toilet paper in my pants.

Fannnntastic.

This is *not* helping my plan for the pool party tomorrow. How am I supposed to make Noah think I'm cool and suave and fun and interesting and mature if I've got toilet paper in my pants!?

And if Noah doesn't think I'm new and improved, the others won't either! People always follow what Noah does. And that's because Noah is nice, adorable, and super funny—but not in the loud, class-clown, "I need attention" way that some people in my school are. Noah doesn't try to be funny—he just is. And he's waaaay more mature than any of the other boys in our grade. Noah is so mature, his parents let him stay up until 11 PM. (He told me that on a bus ride to the Natural History Museum.)

Noah's mom and my dad actually work at the same boring insurance company together, so I like to think Noah and I have some type of unspoken connection.

My plan was to use our parents' jobs as the perfect conversation starter at the party. I'd say something like, *Noah, isn't it random our parents work together?* And he'd respond, *Yeah, so weird. Hey, we should hang out sometime, because we have tons in common!* or something along those lines. Then everyone would see that he likes me, so they would too. It'd be magical. But I wasn't going to follow him around the party looking for attention or anything. That would look desperate. And I'm not desperate—I'm resourceful.

I was just going to show off one of my cool

double flips into the pool, and then he'd come over and—

A horrible thought crosses my mind.

It's a pool party.

As in swimming.

As in bathing suit.

As in how the heck am I going to wear my two-piece bathing suit and get into the pool with the bloody gift I was just delivered?

Oh. No.

This situation has just been kicked up to a level-ten Mom emergency. For reference, the time I tried to cut my own bangs and ended up looking like a sad Chia Pet was only an *eight* on the Mom emergency scale. Clearly, a ten is code red. And there's no time left to waste. I need to get to my bedroom and get her on the phone as soon as possible so I can beg her to come home.

I turn off the sink and take another deep breath before pushing open the bathroom door to hustle to the front door and grab my backpack. Then I make a beeline for my room.

As I pass the doofus twins on the couch, Jamie

mutters under his breath, "Took you long enough." But since I'm mid-crisis, I don't even shoot him a glare in response.

I take the stairs two at a time before lunging into my bedroom and shutting the door behind me.

My phone is an old hand-me-down from Ryan, so it has tiny cracks on the back from being dropped too much, but right now I don't care about any of that. I only care that it is a lifeline to Mom.

I scroll to her cell number and hit the Call button.

It rings once.

It rings twice.

Finally, she answers. "Tahlia?" Her voice sounds distant, like she's taking the call from somewhere underwater.

"Mom!"

"Honey? I can't really hear you." Her voice is garbled. "I—losing service—you—okay?"

"Mom?" I say louder. "You're breaking up, but you need to turn around!"

The line crackles. "What?" she says. "You need a turner hound? What is—"

“No, Mom!” I huff. “Turn around! You need to come home!”

“Oh yeah—Dad picked some up—store. They are—kitchen cabinet,” she answers. It’s clear she has absolutely no idea what I’m saying.

“You. Need. To. Come. Home!” I enunciate each word, loud and slow.

“Tahlia, I—no idea—what you—”

Then the unthinkable happens—the line goes dead. One hundred percent silent. I pull back my phone to look at the screen. It reads, **CALL FAILED**.

I quickly swipe open my messaging app and type her out a text.

PLEASE COME HOME!

But when I hit Send, the text immediately turns red and I get a notification that says, “Not Delivered.”

“No!” I wail and collapse facedown on my bed.

I lie there for a good minute wondering why, oh why, today of all days, the universe is out to get me. First the zit planet, then my first period, then a failed call *well within* the hour Mom said we'd be able to reach her. She specifically said she was reachable for the next hour!

When breathing into the comforter becomes too unbearable, I finally lift myself up and take a deep breath in through my nose and let it out through my mouth—a calming trick I learned from a yoga magazine that was in the waiting room of my doctor's office.

I close my eyes and take another deep breath.

Somehow, I now have to come up with a way to get period products without Mom.

CHAPTER FOUR

A lightbulb switches on in my mind—there's a good chance Mom will have period products in her bathroom that I can use. Maybe if I sneak up there and rifle through her drawers, I can take whatever products she has and use them, until she comes home tomorrow night.

It's not a *great* plan, considering Dad could catch me snooping around in their bathroom and ask what I'm up to, but it's the only real plan I've got.

I poke my head out of my room and discreetly

glance across the hall into my parents' bedroom. Dad isn't inside, so I peer back down the stairs to make sure he's still watching TV with the identical idiots. Thankfully, he is.

I gulp.

If I'm caught rummaging around in my parents' bathroom, I'll have to explain to Dad what I'm looking for, and that would be the death of me. What would I even say?

Oh, don't mind me. Just rummaging around for a big ol' PAD to soak up my brand-new period!

Yeah—no, thank you.

But it's not like I can go all day with toilet paper bunched up in my underwear. I can already feel it starting to tear into smaller pieces that now tickle the side of my leg.

There are no other options. I have to risk being caught.

On the count of three I'll go.

One.

Two.

Three.

Actually, I meant four. I said *four*, right?

Four.

I hold my breath as I cross the threshold into my parents' room. It's spotlessly clean—like always. There are no mountains of clothes like in my room. Mom calls my messy habits "tornado behavior," but I call it "freedom of expression." We agree to disagree.

The door to my parents' en suite bathroom is slightly ajar, so I push it open slowly, just in case it squeaks. Luckily, it's silent. Thank you, quiet, secret-keeping door!

I make sure to close it behind me as I step inside.

My parents' bathroom is, if possible, tidier than their bedroom. Not a single thing is out of place or tilted at the wrong angle. Even their toothbrushes stand at perfect attention in their ceramic holder. Dad will notice that I've been snooping around in here if I am not careful and accidentally move something from its spot.

I carefully drop down to my knees and pull

open the two large drawers under the sink. Everything inside is neatly organized. Makeup bags, weird creams, old-people medications—it's all lined up in order.

My eyes light up when I see a vaguely familiar label on a package that I'm pretty sure I've seen Mom grab from the personal health aisle at the grocery store.

I dig my hands into the package and pull out three wrapped pads. I can practically hear a chorus of angels sing as I look down at the products.

Success! Victory! Triumph! I have found Mom's period stash!

I quickly squish the three pads into my back pocket and hurry out of my parents' bathroom. Before I step into the hall, I check again to make sure no one is coming up the stairs. When I'm positive the coast is clear, I quickly stride across the carpet and into the bathroom I share with my brothers.

I lock the door and plop myself down on the toilet. When I pull down my pants, the folded toilet paper drops from my underwear to the floor.

After I pick up the paper and toss it into the bowl, I unwrap one of the pads from Mom's stash, stick it on my underwear (the way Mrs. Brown taught), and sigh in relief.

That's when another horrible thought crosses my mind.

A terrible, soul-crushing thought.

I'm still not going to be able to swim at Noah's party. Mom's diaper-size pad will soak up all the water and leave everyone standing in a puddle as I waddle around with the entire pool in my drooping suit!

Okay, fine, maybe it won't soak up *all* the pool water, but the pad will 100 percent be noticed by someone when it starts sagging in the suit's bottom. People will think I'm actually wearing a diaper. That'll be ten times worse than people laughing at me for wearing board shorts and goggles last year!

Can you even go into water while you're on your period? No, probably not. Not unless you're looking to re-create one of the scary scenes from *Jaws*. I bet if you went into the sea while you're on your period, a shark would smell the blood, come swimming over, and then—CHOMP! You're shark food.

I don't want to be shark food. Is that really too much to ask?

I need Lily. Pronto. Even though she hasn't gotten her period yet, she'll know what to do. Lily *always* knows what to do. That's why she's my best friend. And as my best friend, she has a BFF duty to be here right now.

I tug up my pants and race out of the bathroom to my bedroom.

After shutting my door, I pull out the two extra pads and stuff them in the far back section of my desk. That way, if the twins come into my bedroom, they won't see the diaper-looking products.

I flop back on the bed and scroll through my phone until I see Lily's name. I use the Call button, and the phone starts ringing.

"Pick up, pick up, pick up!" I mumble to myself.

"Tahlia?" Lily answers on the other end. I

know she's probably curious why I'm calling when I just saw her, but I don't have time to explain. I need her here *yesterday*.

"Lily!" I squeal, happy she's picked up.

"Tahlia!" She mimics my excitement, then asks, "What's up?"

"Can you come over? Like, right now?" I can hear the panic rising in my voice.

"Um, I'm kinda helping my mom with something. Why?" She sounds distracted.

"Just come over and I'll explain," I say. I don't want to tell her about my new arrival on the phone. This is worthy of a face-to-face confession. "Please?"

"I'll need to ask my mom," she says. "You need me *right now* right now?"

"Yes!"

"Okay, one second."

I hear her mumble something to her mom, but I don't hear the response.

"Are you going to show me your one armpit hair again?" she says back into her phone. "My mom says I can come over. I just want to make sure I know what I'm supposed to be hustling over there for."

"*Three* hairs now, thank you very much. And no, it's not that. I don't want to say over the phone. Just come—and hurry."

"Okay, fine. I'll be there in a sec," she says before clicking off.

I stand and toss my phone back onto my bed.

Thankfully, since Lily lives in the same neighborhood, it won't take her very long to walk over.

Having my best friend live within walking distance is totally divine. We are always at each other's house, especially during the summer. I lost count of all the days and nights we stayed at each other's place last summer. But at this point, I'd say we've spent more nights having sleepovers than not.

When Jackie was still part of our group, our neighbors used to call us the Three Amigos, but I think the Perfect Pair sounds better anyway, or at least good enough for now. We can always think of a new group name when we win over Noah and other classmates.

Lily always knows the perfect thing to say to make me feel better or laugh, or just generally enjoy being with her.

Moral of the story: Lily is amazing.

And even though I know I'll have to wait only a few minutes for her arrival, I can't stop myself from pacing around my bedroom.

Back and forth.

Back and forth.

I wonder if all the pacing will make my period come out quicker. Maybe if I'm able to drain it all out today, I won't have it at Noah's party. I stop my pacing and shake my hips, but I know it's just wishful thinking. Mrs. Brown said periods usually last around a week. A full bloody week!

I start pacing again.

The two-piece bathing suit I picked out for Noah's party is draped over my desk chair in the corner. It's taunting me. I know it is. It's saying,

Oh, look at me, with my cute yellow stripes and ruffles! Aren't I adorable? Too bad you'll never get to wear me in the pool with Noah!

Right when I decide I'm going to chuck the evil bathing suit out my bedroom window, there's a loud knock on the front door downstairs.

"I got it!" I shout to no one in particular as I bounce down the stairs.

I chuckle to myself at the irony of my yelling "I got it!" to all the menfolk in the house when I have indeed gotten *it*. They'll never know what *it* I mean. Ha!

Downstairs, the twins are still on the couch watching TV, but Dad is no longer with them. He's probably gone off to bumble around in his office. Dads like to do that—bumble around. At least that's what Mom says. *Dad is bumbling around in the garage again.*

When I reach the door, I fling it open to see Lily waiting on the porch. She's changed out of her pants and into jean shorts. Even though I'm taller than she is, her jean shorts make her seem even longer and more string-beany than I am.

She wastes no time in cutting to the chase.

"What's the big emergency?" she asks with a curious expression.

Even though Lily is nice, she has a no-nonsense attitude. She always means business when she sets her mind to something. It's great when it's in my favor—like the time I randomly mentioned that my favorite cheese snacks were no longer being carried by the local grocery store, so she declared we were going to spend the day biking into town to check all the stores until we found them. When the first few stores were a bust, I was ready to give up, but she put her foot down and said we had to keep looking. We ended up finding the snacks hours later at the gas station and then ate them all afternoon. It was glorious.

But it's not as great when it means she becomes stubborn—like the time she insisted we watch her favorite movie, *Jurassic Park*, again, even though I've told her that old movie freaks me out. I wanted to see something new that didn't have giant dinosaurs running around, but *oh, no*, she crossed her arms and pouted until I gave in.

"Please don't tell me I came all the way over here to look at your chin zit," Lily says.

"Ugh, don't remind me about pimple planet," I groan. "Come on," I say, tugging on her arm. "Let's go up to my room. I'll explain everything there."

She follows me up the stairs to my bedroom, where I promptly shut the door behind her.

Lily crosses her legs on the edge of my bed and looks at me expectantly, waiting for me to spill the beans about why I called her over.

I've imagined having this very conversation with Lily many times before. Since Lily has always been a little less developed (as the adults would say) than I am, I've always figured I'd get mine first. However, in my imagination, when I tell Lily I've gotten my period, it's something I brag about, not something that's an utter disaster.

Already my period is ruining all expectations.

Lily raises an eyebrow, probably wondering what's taking me so long to explain why she's here. Not wanting to drag out the suspense any longer, I sit next to her on the bed and quietly announce, "Lily, I *got* it."

She narrows her eyes at me. "Got what?"

I shoot a glance to my bedroom door, double-checking that it's all the way closed and no one in the hallway can hear me. "I got my *period*," I say softly.

"Whoa." She looks impressed, and her eyes widen in surprise. "Really? What did it feel like?" She leans forward.

I pause, considering. I hadn't really thought about what it felt like. I've had much more important, pool-related problems to worry about.

"It was weird, I guess," I answer. "Almost like a gurgling in my lower stomach. I can't really explain it."

"Strange." Lily nods her head with a captivated smile. "Jackie said it felt like she peed her pants and—"

"Yes, I know what Jackie said," I snap.

"Jeez, I'm only repeating it," Lily shoots back.

"Well, I was there when she said it. I remember."

Lily rolls her eyes and sighs, "Whatever."

"Anyways"—I wave it off, trying to move past all the Jackie talk—"now I've *literally* got a code-red problem." I let my head fall into my hands.

"What do you mean? Did it go through your underwear and stain your pants?" Lily looks down at my jeans.

"No, no, the pants were spared." I blow out a breath. "Thank God."

"Do you have cramps?"

"I don't think so."

"I think you'd know. They'd hurt," she declares, as if she's the expert on period cramps.

"Well, then I don't."

"Then what's the issue?"

I groan. "Noah's pool party tomorrow! How am I supposed to get in the water and show off my new two-piece suit now?"

Lily lies back on my bed. "Oh man. Good point. Won't the blood swirl out into the water?"

"I don't know!" I throw up my hands.

She takes a deep breath and adds, "And even if you don't want to go in the water, someone might push you in."

"I know!" I practically wail.

Lily gives me a sympathetic expression. "That really sucks."

I moan in agreement and lie down next to her. "What should I do?"

She doesn't answer right away, but I can tell by the way she's scrunched her nose that wheels are spinning in her head.

Suddenly, she shoots back up into her sitting position. "Tampons!"

"What about them?" I narrow my eyes at her.

Obviously, I've heard of tampons before. I just don't see how they could help in this situation. Weren't tampons something you had to work up to after years of using pads? Tampons seem way too complicated for a period first-timer.

Lily starts talking very fast. "My cousin, the one who lives in Florida, she once told me that when she's on"—she lowers her voice—"that *time of the month* and has to go to swim practice, she uses tampons!"

"Really? Your cousin swims with tampons in? You can do that?" I raise an eyebrow.

Lily bounces on the bed. "Yes!" She stops bouncing. "At least I think so."

“Let’s look it up to make sure,” I say, walking over to my laptop—another hand-me-down from one of the twins.

Lily flops to her stomach as I bring the laptop over to the bed from my desk. I open it up and type in my password—FrenchToast4Life. The home screen appears, and I click open a new window.

“What should I google? I don’t want, like, gross things popping up.” I wrinkle my nose and remember a time when Lily and I googled something we thought was innocent. It was not.

“Just write ‘swimming with periods,’ ” Lily suggests.

I type it in and click the first link. Thankfully, no weird images appear on the screen.

Lily points to some text below the link. “See! That article says to just use a tampon while swimming.”

I keep scrolling and click on another link.

“But this one says I don’t need to wear anything because of the water pressure. I won’t get my period in water,” I say.

“Really? That doesn’t seem right.” Lily clucks

her tongue. "Are you sure that's not just one of those old wives' tales Mrs. Brown warned us about in class? Like that you shouldn't exercise on your period?"

I chew the inside of my cheek. "Let's check one more link to be positive," I say as I start scrolling again.

An official-looking website catches my eye, so I click the link. After scanning the first few paragraphs, I find the information I want and read aloud, "While the water pressure will temporarily stop the flow of a period, the use of a tampon or menstrual cup is recommended to protect against accidental leaks while swimming. Additionally, a tampon or cup will stop period discharge while entering and exiting the water."

"What the heck is a menstrual cup?" Lily asks.

I frown. "No idea. I don't think Mrs. Brown covered that one."

"But at least I was right about the tampons! You can swim with them."

"True!" I let out a sigh of relief before closing

the laptop and facing Lily. "So, do you have a tampon I can borrow?" I pause. "Well, *have*. Not borrow. I won't be giving it back."

Lily raises an eyebrow. "Why would *I* have a tampon? You know I haven't started it yet."

"I know, but maybe your mom took you shopping to get some products beforehand, just in case."

"Nope," she answers and shakes her head. "Not yet. The doctor says I'll be a late bloomer."

I groan.

"Maybe your mom has some," she suggests.

"Already looked. She only has pads." I say the word *pads* with a sneer.

Lily rests her chin in her palm, thinking. "You could go buy some?"

I cringe.

The thought of buying a box of tampons at our local grocery store is not appealing at all. The grocery store is the only store within walking distance of my house, and my parents drag me along shopping with them there all the time. People *know* me at that store. I don't want Mary Ann, the cashier, or Thomas, the grocery bagger, knowing my *puberty affairs*.

"I don't know…" I trail off.

Lily makes a face.

I cross my arms. "What?"

"I mean, you could always ask Jackie for some. You know she has them."

I let out an annoyed huff. "Why is it always 'Jackie, Jackie, Jackie'? She doesn't even like us, Lily. I am *not* going to ask her for tampons."

She frowns. "I think she still likes us, she just…"

"She just what?"

Lily shrugs. "Wants to be popular."

Her comment stings more than I think she means it to. She's basically saying we're not popular, which hurts—even though I know she's not exactly wrong.

I try to shrug it off. Besides, if Noah's pool party goes the way I want it to, then maybe we *will* be. That's the whole reason it has to go perfectly.

"Well, I'm not asking her," I say.

“What other options do you have?”

I give her a weak, hopeful smile. “We could sneak into Noah’s backyard in the middle of the night and drain his pool so he’s forced to postpone his party until after my period?”

She crosses her arms. “Nice try.”

“Fine,” I mumble and walk over to my dresser, where I flip open the decorative jewelry box that holds my savings. A little ballerina twirls in the middle of the box once the lid is open. I’m probably a bit too old for the pink and frilly ballerina box, but I haven’t gotten around to getting a new one. I still like this jewelry box, but I think the new and improved Tahlia should start putting her money in a purse—something like what the twins’ girlfriends have when they come over. It’d be nice to have a purse for more than just my phone. Besides, now I’ll have to start carrying pads around anyway.

I dig out the twenty-dollar bill (the one that Grandma Judy slipped into my birthday card this year) from the bottom of the box, under old nail polish and ChapStick.

Grandma Judy probably never thought her

twenty-dollar gift would be used for emergency tampons. Well, guess what, Grandma Judy? That makes two of us. I was hoping to save up for something a little bit more special than *this*.

Lily stands up from my bed and twiddles her thumbs. "Tahlia, by the way, about next year, I've been meaning to tell you—"

"Wait, do you think twenty dollars will be enough?" I interrupt. I need to make sure we have more than enough cash.

She nods. "Yes, plenty, but—"

"Was that Lily who knocked at the door?" Dad calls up the stairs loudly from wherever he's been bumbling around downstairs.

"Yes!" I shout back through my closed door.

"Come down and say hi!" he yells.

I pocket the money and open my door. "We're coming!" I shout. Then I turn to Lily and tell her, "You're coming with me to the store, right? I don't think I can buy them alone." I shudder at the thought.

Lily is frowning at me.

"What?" I ask.

"Nothing." She rolls her eyes and exhales. "Come on," she says and pushes herself up off the bed. "Let's go say hi to your dad."

Lily and I make our way back downstairs. As we pass the twins on the couch, Lily waves at them.

"Hi, Ryan. Hi, Jamie," she says, smiling.

"Hey, Lily," they say back in unison.

Lily's cheeks burn red.

I know she thinks they're cute. Every time Jamie or Ryan so much as throws her a passing glance, she giggles and clams up. I try not to gag when I think about it. My brothers are the grossest human beings to have ever walked the earth. The thought of Lily, my best friend, having a crush on them is revolting.

"Hey, Lily," Dad says as he walks into the living room from the kitchen. "Good to see you."

"Hi, Mr. Wilkins," Lily answers politely.

"Getting excited to be a big sister?"

Lily politely nods. "Mhmm, yes."

"Big changes, big changes." Dad crosses his arms. "You know, I saw your dad the other day, and he told me that your family—"

I have to stop him mid-sentence before he pulls us into an hour-long conversation. “Dad, we’re going to Lily’s house for a bit,” I lie. “Be home later.”

“Oh, okay then.” He nods. “Have fun.”

“Thanks!” I say over my shoulder as I lead Lily out the front door.

CHAPTER FIVE

Our neighborhood is a small suburban square made up of five streets running north-south and five streets running east-west—smack-dab in the middle of Pennsylvania. It's a new development. In fact, my family is only the second family to live in our house. I don't remember it, but my parents say that when we first moved to town, they were still building the last street of houses.

I like living in our neighborhood, for the most part. It means we have a big yard, and I'm close to Lily, but one bad thing about living in a new development is that a lot of stores still haven't opened up within walking distance. Lily and I can bike a few places, but every time my family wants to go somewhere other than the small local grocery store, it's a complete circus, because the twins always fight for who gets to sit in the front seat. When I get my license, I'll finally be able to go somewhere interesting without having to be chauffeured by the idiot twins.

There were once plans to build a strip mall next to our neighborhood, but for some reason, it never happened. Now it's just bulldozed land that kids use to make dirt-biking paths. Lily, Jackie, and I used to follow my brothers out there and try to copy their bike tricks, but after Jackie toppled over the front of her handlebars and sprained her wrist, my parents said we weren't allowed to go without supervision. But it was fun while it lasted.

The only small grocery store near us is at the main entrance of the housing development, so Lily and I turn left once we step outside my front door. It's only a few blocks away, but right now the distance seems farther than a trip to Madagascar.

Since it is a sunny Friday afternoon, a few of our neighbors are out mowing their lawns, walking their dogs, and playing in their front yards. They all wave and smile as we pass, completely oblivious that they are some of the first people to greet the new, *mature* Tahlia. They should feel honored.

I wonder if I look any different to them. Can they all tell just by looking at me that I've crossed into the land of Menstruation Nation?

Lily and I kick a rock back and forth along the sidewalk as we make our way down the street. She's quieter than usual, but I don't press her on it. I bet she's probably feeling weird that I got my period before she did. I remember being jealous when Jackie told us about getting hers.

After we walk for about ten minutes, the grocery store's sign finally comes into view ahead of us: **MOE'S FAMILY GROCERY STORE**.

It's written in an old-timey font to look quaint, as if the store has been here forever. I'd believe it too if I didn't know the truth about our brand-new area of town.

A bell above the store door chimes as we walk in, and Mary Ann, the cashier, greets us with a smile. She has curly red hair and multicolored nails and is wearing a blue apron.

"Need any help finding anything today, ladies?" she asks.

Mary Ann is one of those people who are permanently friendly. Usually I like her cheerful personality, but today I just want her to leave us alone. The less attention we draw, the better.

"No, thank you!" I say back with a sweet smile. As long as we blend in with the other few customers in the store, we won't look suspicious.

Lily takes a step toward the aisle labeled **PERSONAL HEALTH & BATHROOM SUPPLIES**, and I softly grab her arm.

"Let's not make a beeline for *that* section," I say under my breath. "Let's just go aisle by aisle so it looks like we're buying regular things. I don't want it to be obvious why we're here."

Lily's mouth forms an understanding O, and she nods.

We meander into the first aisle, closest to the

register. Without really looking at price or brand, I reach up and grab a box of crackers.

"You're hungry?" Lily asks.

I keep my voice lowered. "No, but I'm not going up to the counter and only buying tampons!" I look over my shoulders to make sure no one is listening. "I'm going to just buy a bunch of random things to mix in with the tampons so Mary Ann won't specifically notice the *hot-ticket item*."

"Yeah, that makes sense," Lily agrees, and she grabs a package of cookies.

We make our way through the store, randomly selecting items until our hands are nearly full. When we get to the aisle with the tampons, we slowly stroll down it as if this aisle were like any other aisle.

As we pass the section with all the *menstruation products* (yuck again to that phrase), I try not to look directly at them. I don't want someone to see me and think I'm seriously considering buying a box.

Without even looking at the label, I casually grab the closest tampon box and tuck it under my arm. Then, carrying the random items we've picked up and the tampon box, Lily and I make our way back to the counter, where Mary Ann happily waits behind the checkout register with a scanner.

We give her big, toothy grins. I carefully set down each item on the conveyor belt and make sure it looks like we took a lot of time and care picking everything out. When I get to the box of tampons, I place it directly behind a box of Fruity Flakes cereal, making it hard for Mary Ann to see.

Mary Ann begins to scan each item, and Thomas, the bagger, walks over to put them in a large brown bag. It's a slow dance of scan, bag, scan, bag. Time seems to slow down as Mary Ann gets closer and closer to grabbing the tampon box, and I have to force myself not to stare directly at it. I'm pretty sure that if I make eye contact with the tampon box, my eyes will melt into tiny puddles on the floor from this cringe-worthy moment.

Is it possible to explode from mortification? Because I think I'm about to.

When she finally grabs the box, I hold my breath, anticipating her shooting me a curious look any second.

Thankfully, the look doesn't come. Instead,

Mary Ann claps her hands together and says, "That'll be twenty-five dollars and forty-seven cents."

Lily and I exchange a worried glance. We have only my twenty-dollar bill from Grandma Judy.

"Um, I think we're going to put a few things back," I say, as I sheepishly slide a tube of toothpaste off the counter.

Thomas has already bagged everything else, so I have to awkwardly peer into the brown bag and pretend to think over which items I want to put back. I make my best pretend-thinking face. If I don't look like I'm thinking over the items, it'll be obvious that I really don't care about anything other than the box of tampons.

Hmm, pretend decisions, pretend decisions. Do I put back the crackers or the cookies?

Mary Ann looks over my shoulder and into the bag too.

"Oh, you know what?" Mary Ann exclaims, and I watch in horror as she reaches into the brown bag and pulls out the tampons. "I think these are actually on sale. Let me check!"

She holds the tampon box out like a prized vegetable at the county fair and reaches for the price-check microphone.

My stomach drops.

Oh God, I hope she's not—

"Can I get a sale-price check on aisle seven?" she chirps into the mic.

My mouth goes dry and a wave of embarrassment-caused nausea washes over me. I choke back the rising bubbles in my throat.

Welp, she did it. She really did it. She's called over the manager to come take a look at my tampon box.

Lily gives me a sympathetic look.

Please let me evaporate into thin air. I would give my left arm to have the power of invisibility this very second. Heck, I'd give my right arm to be anywhere else, and that's the arm I actually use!

Mr. Dufman, the store manager, hustles over to the cashier station. He's a tall, gangly man with small ears and a balding head.

"You need a price check?" he asks Mary Ann.

I nervously rub the back of my neck. It's slick

with sweat, so I have to quickly wipe my hand down the front of my pants. Great, I guess I stress-sweat now. That's another *awesome* thing I can add to the list of not-so-fun things that happened to me today.

Mary Ann holds up the tampon box, and I can feel my face drain of color. I've had a good life, but clearly this is where it ends. I was hoping to live a little longer, but I'm pretty sure my body will give out before the end of their conversation.

"It scanned for five dollars, but I'm pretty sure I saw a sale sticker in the aisle for these," Mary Ann explains, holding up the tampon box and causing me to die a slow, painful death with each word.

Mr. Dufman scratches his head. "Oh yeah. Those tampons are four bucks this week. Try to re-scan."

I'm not sure he could've said the word *tampons* any louder if he tried. He might as well have just shouted it into a microphone, for Pete's sake. Now the entire store knows exactly what I'm buying.

Mary Ann turns to look at Lily and me. "Four

dollars—that's a pretty good deal. You want to get two boxes?"

Aaand that's it. I've made up my mind. I'm never shopping here again. I don't even care if my parents try to drag me in. I will purposefully catch the measles before entering this store ever again.

I'm too embarrassed to answer.

Mary Ann stares at us, waiting. She lifts an eyebrow.

"Just the one box is fine," Lily says, nervously chuckling.

A massive weight lifts from my chest. Man, how could I live without Lily? She is my saint, my hero, my—

Lily turns to me. "Actually, did you want a second box, Tahlia? It *is* a good deal."

Traitor!

"Um, no. No, thank you," I manage to squeak.

Mary Ann nods and punches a few buttons on her register. "With the tampons on sale and without the toothpaste, your new total is nineteen dollars and forty-seven cents," she states cheerfully, as if she seriously expects me to be happy about this entire transaction.

I quickly pull out the twenty-dollar bill from my pocket and slap it down on the counter.

"You can keep the change," I blurt as I lunge for the handles of the brown bag and hustle out of the store. Lily quickly follows me.

"Have a nice day!" Mary Ann calls after us. However, thanks to her, there is zero chance of that happening.

Once we are in the parking lot, I swivel around to face Lily. "You completely threw me under the bus in there!"

She gives me a sheepish shrug. "Well, it is a good deal, and you'll need more tampons next month anyways."

I have no time for a witty retort, because just then I see something that makes my stomach drop to the pavement.

Noah and Jackie (why is it *always* her?) have stepped out from around the corner and are walking our way. All my plans for tomorrow will be ruined if they see me carrying a box of tampons.

Since Lily has her back to them and can't see them quickly approaching, I whisper, "Stop talking about tampons!"

She puts her hands on her hips and raises an eyebrow. "Huh? Why?"

Before I can explain, Noah and Jackie come up beside us. Lily's eyes instantly flash with understanding.

"Hey, guys." Noah gives us a small wave, and I have to stop myself from melting into the sidewalk from his adorableness.

"Hi!" Lily and I say in unison.

Jackie smiles at us, but it feels like her smile is saying, *Aren't you jealous I live close to Noah and get to hang out with him after school?*

It's then that I remember the massive, life-destroying pimple on my chin.

Oh my sweet bejeezus.

I feel my face flush bright red and the back of my neck go hot. My hand flies up to my chin in an awkward attempt to cover the zit from Noah and Jackie's view. There is no doubt I now look like a crazy person holding the bottom half of my face.

I mean, honestly, could this day get any worse?

Answer: No. Not one bit.

If lightning were to strike down and zap me into millions of charred little pieces, I'd accept my fate with open arms if it meant I didn't have to deal with pimples or periods ever again.

"You're coming to my pool party tomorrow, yeah?" Noah flashes us one of his magazine-cover smiles.

Must. Not. Swoon. Over. Popular. Kid. In. Parking. Lot.

"Yes! Can't wait," Lily says. "It'll be super fun."

"Yeah, super fun," Jackie agrees, as if we hadn't already talked with her about going to his party at school.

"You're coming too, right, Tahlia?" Noah turns to face me.

Please don't see my pimple. Please don't see my pimple.

I nod while keeping my hand on my chin. "Oh yes, definitely," I say through my fingers.

"Nice." He smiles. "Good."

I try to think of something interesting or witty

or cool or anything to say back, but my mouth has gone dry.

"I love those cookies," he says.

Seeing my confused expression, he adds, "Those cookies in your bag." Noah points to the brown bag I'm holding. Sticking out the top is the cookie package Lily picked out. And right below it, poking out to the side, is—you guessed it—the tampon box.

I resist the urge to wail, *Seriously!?*

At this point, lightning can't strike me down fast enough.

I try to move the bag behind my left leg and a bit farther out of their view without the motion being noticed.

"They're my favorite too!" Jackie exclaims.

They're not. I know for a fact that her favorite cookies are the soft double-chocolate-chunk cookies from the farmers market. She made Lily and me bike with her to that market *loads* of times during the summer of fifth grade just so she could get those cookies.

"No way!" Noah gives her a high five.

Lily and I exchange a glance, and I try to think of something interesting to say that would get me a high five from Noah, but I draw a blank.

Jackie turns to Lily. “So, Lily, are you so excited about everything? I would be. When you told me, I was like, *whoa*. I could not imagine going—”

“Yeah, I’m excited,” Lily answers quickly.

I give Lily a confused glance. It’s not like her to interrupt people, especially not Jackie. And what in the world did Lily tell her? It makes a suspicious tingle run down my spine, especially since Jackie now has a weird grin on her face.

If only I could figure out what Jackie was about to say. I’d ask her directly if I actually liked her. Which I do *not*.

Noah motions to the store behind us. “Well, we better go. My mom asked me to pick up a few things before the party tomorrow. But I’ll see you then!”

“Right, okay,” I say, chuckling, but it comes out muffled behind my hand. “We’ll see you tomorrow!”

They head toward the store, leaving Lily and me standing alone on the sidewalk again.

When I'm positive they are out of hearing range, I let out a huff and say, "What was she talking about?"

"Huh?" Lily watches them walk into the store.

"Jackie—what was she talking about? What did you tell her?"

"Oh"—she scratches her arm—"I think she's just talking about the new baby." She looks down at her shoes and kicks a loose pebble. "She knows my mom is pregnant."

I narrow my eyes at her. I don't like the thought of Jackie knowing something about Lily that I don't. "You're acting funny."

"No, I'm not," she says defensively.

"Whatever." I roll my eyes. "Come on. Let's just head back so I can stop carrying this bag and get my chin away from public view."

CHAPTER SIX

Ten minutes later, Lily and I march back up my driveway and push open the front door.

As soon as we step inside, Dad, who is riffling through the mail on the kitchen table, looks up at us and says, “Back so soon? Thought you were spending the afternoon at Lily’s.”

Whoops.

My stomach sinks. I’d forgotten about that little white lie.

I rack my brain for another lie. “Oh, no. We were just...”

Nothing convincing comes to mind. This is what it has come down to—coming up with lies to cover lies. Having a period is becoming a dangerous game.

"Just grabbing my phone charger," Lily chimes in. "Tahlia and I have different phones, so I can't use hers." She looks down at the large bag I'm carrying. "And a few other things," she adds.

"Of course." Dad rolls his eyes and chuckles to himself. "Because you couldn't possibly hang out with each other without charged phones. You know, when I was a kid—"

"Mhmm, sure, Dad," I quickly say and motion to Lily to follow me up the stairs. If we show any signs of weakness, Dad will launch into a full monologue about his tragic life-on-the-prairie childhood without a phone.

We hustle to my bedroom and quickly shut the door behind us. I dump the brown bag onto my bed, and the cookies, crackers, shampoo, cereal, and tampon box tumble across the comforter.

Lily grabs the cookie package, pulls it open, picks one out, and begins to munch.

I reach for the tampon box and read the front label. " 'Pack of ten. Regular. Unscented.' " I look up from the box. "There are such things as scented tampons?"

Lily shrugs. "I guess so."

"Yuck."

Lily leans closer to read the tampon box over my shoulder. "What's a 'cardboard applicator'?" She points to a sentence at the bottom of the package that reads "Easy-to-use cardboard applicator," and says, "I don't remember Mrs. Brown talking about applicators."

"Looks like I'm about to find out," I say and stand, box in hand, ready to slay the tampon dragon in the bathroom.

"Wait!" Lily takes the box from my hand and rips open the top. "Let's read the instructions. You know, just as a refresher."

"Good idea," I agree and pull out the folded instruction packet to flatten it across my comforter.

Lily points to the top-left corner and reads, " 'Step one: Wash your hands.' "

"Duh," I say, nodding. Then I read the next line. " 'Step two: Get into a relaxed and comfortable position.' "

Step two also includes two images, one with a woman sitting with wide knees on the toilet and the other with a woman standing with one leg on the seat.

"I think I'll just sit," I decide. "Balancing like that on one leg doesn't look too relaxed."

" 'Step three,' " Lily continues. " 'Insert tampon into vagina with cardboard applicator.' "

The image next to step three is a cross-sectional diagram of the tampon sliding in at an angle.

I read. " 'Step four: Push the inner tube of the applicator until it meets the outer tube.' " I turn to Lily. "Did Mrs. Brown say anything about tubes?"

"Only the fallopian tubes," she says, making a face.

Luckily, the image next to step four explains a bit more, and it shows a hand pushing the back half of the tampon tube into the front half.

Lily keeps reading. "'Step five: Discard applicator. You should not feel any discomfort. If not properly inserted, remove and start again with fresh tampon. Change tampon every eight hours or when needed.'"

"Sounds simple enough," I say.

"And finally, 'Step six: Wash your hands.'" Lily makes a face at me. "Yuck, I would hope you'd wash your hands after that."

"Obviously." I fold up the instructions. "All right, I think I'm ready."

Lily stands up from the bed and jokingly gives me a military salute. "Good luck in battle, soldier."

My stomach clenches at the sentence. It's something Jackie used to say whenever one of us would stop playing and run to the bathroom. It *used* to be funny.

I pull out a tampon from the box and hug it to my chest.

"Here goes nothing," I huff before opening my bedroom door and scurrying to the bathroom across the hall.

I step inside and make sure to lock the bathroom door behind me. Unfortunately, I share this bathroom with Jamie and Ryan, so their dirty clothes and used towels are piled up in large heaps on the floor. The sight of my brothers' gross socks doesn't give me the peaceful and relaxed mood I would like, but it'll have to do.

I wash my hands before tugging down my pants and sitting on the toilet. I rip off the used pad from my underwear, roll it up, and bury it at the bottom of the trash.

At first, my fingers struggle to open the tampon package. When I finally tear it open, relief floods through me. How pathetic would I be if I couldn't even open the dang thing?

I roll the tampon between my thumb and index finger as I take a deep breath.

I can do this. How hard could it even be? If *Jackie* can do it, I can do it.

With tampon in hand, I lean forward on the seat, reach down, and give it a go.

Only something's not right.

It's not entering like the instruction packet described. It's not sliding or gliding or going anywhere at all. I'm just jabbing myself.

I try again.

The cardboard applicator sticks to my skin in a way that is not at all helpful for sliding. I must have the angle all wrong.

I try and I try and I try. But no luck.

There's a soft knock at the door. "Tahlia? How's it going in there?" Lily asks. I can hear the concern in her voice. I know it shouldn't be taking this long to stick in a tampon.

"It won't go in!" I whisper back.

There's a pause.

"What do you mean, 'It won't go in'?"

"What do you think I mean!?"

"I don't know!"

I look at the tampon in my hand. "Slide another one under the door," I say to her. "Maybe this one doesn't work. It could be defective."

Lily pushes a new wrapped tampon under the door, and I grab it off the bathroom's tiled floor.

I unwrap it and try again. This time I push a bit harder, but that only makes me wince. Just in case by some miracle I've lined up the angle correctly, I push the inner tube into the outer tube, which turns out to be a stupid thing to do. It only causes the cotton tampon to pop out and drop into the bowl with a little plop.

I groan in frustration.

"Slide another!" I instruct Lily.

Another tampon appears under the door.

I try it.

Still no luck.

I try another. Then another. And another. And another. And another.

Every time I think I've lined it up correctly, I push the inner tube and then the tampon plops into the toilet bowl—obviously not where it's supposed to be.

What a nightmare.

I lean back against toilet seat, defeated. "Lily, I'm telling you. The tampons won't go in!"

I can hear the rustle of her unfolding the instructions again. She's probably rereading to make sure we didn't miss a step. "But it has to go in!" she says under the door. "It's designed to go in! Maybe we missed a step?"

"I don't know! I don't think I did—the angle is just all wrong. I can't get it to slide!"

"Try bending over," Lily suggests.

"It definitely did not say to *bend over* in the instructions. It said get in a *relaxed and comfortable* position. Bending over is not relaxed!" I protest.

"You might as well try."

"Fine," I grump. "Can I have another one?"

She sends another tampon under the door. I glare at it before reluctantly picking it up. After a few long seconds, I stand, bend over, and start poking around.

But of course it's useless.

"No, this isn't working, and I feel like an idiot," I moan. "I'm sitting back down and trying the old way again. Can you slide me another one?"

There's a beat of silence from Lily's side of the door.

"Lily?"

"Tahlia, that's it! I just slid you the last one! There are no more in the box!"

My heart stops in my chest. "*Please* tell me you are joking," I beg.

"I told you we should've gotten a second box," Lily scolds.

I close my eyes as they begin to water.

This is *not* going according to plan. None of this is going according to plan at all.

If Mom were here, she'd know what to do. She'd rub my back and whip out a second box of tampons, which she would have just *known* that I needed to buy. And she would have paid for them, so I'd still have Grandma Judy's money tucked away for future use.

And now, on top of that, there is a very real chance I'll have to go to the pool party without knowing how to use a tampon. What will I even say?

Yes, I know I got in the water last year, but I've actually recently developed a water allergy. Sorry!

That's even worse than being known as the weird board-shorts-and-goggles kid!

Mom just had to be gone this weekend, didn't she? She left without a second thought that her daughter might need her urgently. I'm going to give her a serious talking-to about the timing of her work trips when she gets back tomorrow night.

I sniffle.

"You okay?" Lily lightly taps on the bathroom door.

I use my sleeve to wipe my eyes and nose. "I'm fine!" I call back. I know Lily wouldn't make fun of me for crying or anything, but I don't want to have to admit I'm upset because Mom is gone. I'm supposed to be new and improved, and crying in defeat does not fit in with the new, *mature* Tahlia.

I take a deep breath and focus on just getting out of the bathroom.

Since I already took off my used pad, and the two remaining pads from Mom's bathroom are hidden in my desk, I have to fold up toilet paper and stick it in my underwear again. Then I pull up my pants and shove the cardboard applicators to the bottom of the trash can.

After washing my hands, I open the door. Lily gives me a sympathetic frown as we walk back to my room.

"What do I do now?" I moan. "My body is a freak of nature that won't accept tampons!"

Lily puts her arm around my shoulders. "Oh, stop. You know that's not it. There just has to be some trick to putting them in. You'll learn."

"But now I'm out of tampons to learn with." I flop onto my bed.

"Yeah, that's not great," Lily sighs with a nod. "Looks like we have to go back to the store."

I make a face of disgust. "No way. Nuh-uh. Never going to happen. I will never be going back to that store again. Besides, I don't have any more money."

"But it's the only store within walking distance! And we could ask your dad for more money."

I sit up. "Lily, I'm not being dramatic when I say I will die if Dad ever finds out about this. He'd probably ask me tons of questions. I would not survive that humiliating situation."

"Whatever," she says and crosses her arms. "Then what do you suggest we do? Since my ideas don't seem to be good."

I jump up and begin to pace my room.

When nothing comes to mind, I collapse into the chair by the window that overlooks the street.

Outside my house, Sophie, the popular sixteen-year-old who lives next door, is walking her dog named Willow, a gigantic, slobbery mastiff. Willow is pulling on the leash so hard, it looks like he is trying to choke himself.

Sophie's long hair bounces in a way my frizzy curls can only hope to achieve. It's like she's practically walking in slow motion as her hair floats gracefully behind her.

I can't help but stare. I bet when Sophie first got her period, *she* knew how to use a tampon. When she got her period, I bet she was more than prepared and didn't have to wad up toilet paper to shove in her underwear. Sophie probably went into a pool the same day she got her period with no trouble at all.

That's when an idea pops into my head. A lovely, devious idea.

"I think I know how we can get more tampons!" I exclaim as I spring from the chair.

CHAPTER SEVEN

At my sudden excitement, Lily jolts in surprise. "What? What is it?"

I point out the window at Sophie and Willow. "Sophie—you know, the girl who lives next door? I bet she has tampons!"

Lily's face lights up. "That's brilliant! We can ask her for a few, and maybe she could give you a few tips on how to use them!"

I make a face. I hate the idea of asking Sophie for "tips." That'll make Sophie think we have no idea what we're doing. Which, to be fair, we don't, but I don't want perfect-hair Sophie knowing that. What if she tells someone we came to her for help? That'd be so embarrassing!

Lily raises an eyebrow, not catching on to my mischievous idea.

I say, "That's not exactly what I'm thinking..."

"What?" Lily narrows her eyes at me, knowing I'm about to say something she won't agree with.

"Well, uh"—I twirl my thumbs—"you know, Sophie is friends with my brothers, and they talk all the time."

"So?" Lily crosses her arms.

"*So*," I say, widening my eyes, "I don't want to risk Sophie telling them that I've started my period."

Lily rolls her eyes. "Right. As if that's the number one thing Sophie wants to talk about with your brothers. Your period."

I put up my hands. "I'm just saying she might accidentally let slip it out!"

"And?" She puts her hands on her hips.

I sigh. "You don't have brothers. You don't understand. Jamie and Ryan won't let an opportunity to make fun of me slide!" I look down at my hands and lower my voice. "Once, a few years ago, Jamie tickled me so hard that I peed my pants." I close my eyes, remembering that terrible day. "They thought it was so funny, they even made up a stupid nickname because of it—Professor Pee Pants."

Lily cracks a small smile. "Oh! I've wondered why they sometimes call you the Professor."

I scowl at her. It only makes her smile wider.

"I do *not* want Professor Pee Pants to become Professor Period Pantaloons or Bloody Bloomers. That'd be horrific!"

"I'm so glad I'm an only child," she muses, but then her face drops. "Well, for a little while longer, at least." There's a beat of silence between us before she adds, "Actually, about that. I've been meaning to tell you—"

"Wait—that's it!" I exclaim, another idea springing to mind. "You don't have any brothers to make fun of you! Why don't you just ask Sophie for the tampons? Then she'll think they're for you!"

Lily rolls her eyes. "Oh, sure. Let *me* take the fall."

"Exactly!" I laugh.

She shakes her head no. "I don't really want your brothers calling me Professor Bloody Pants or whatever either."

I sigh. "Yeah, fair enough. Brothers are the worst."

"Have any better plans?" Lily asks. "Other than letting me get thrown under the tampon bus." She gives me a pointed look.

My mouth curls into a mischievous smile.

"Why do I just know I'm not going to like this?" Lily mutters under her breath.

I ignore her and explain my idea. "Okay, what if we knock on her door and say we accidentally kicked a soccer ball or something into her backyard and were wondering if we could grab it. Then, when she lets us in, one of us pretends they suddenly really have to go to the bathroom, while the other pretends to search out in the yard. While you're in the bathroom pretending to pee, you can just snoop around and grab a few of her tampons!"

"Why are you assuming I'll be the one snooping in the bathroom?"

“Fine. *I’ll* be the one in the bathroom.”

She nods. “Yes, you will. Because it’s *your* crazy plan.”

I clap my hands together. “So, you’ll do it? You’ll distract her in the backyard while I look in her bathroom for a tampon?”

“I don’t know . . .” She trails off as she pulls her phone out of her back pocket to check the time. “I kinda should be getting home. I have to—”

“Lily, you can’t leave now!” I groan and take her hands in mine. “I’m nowhere closer to getting into Noah’s pool tomorrow!” Then I add, “Please stay?” I pout my lower lip.

“Fine.” Lily reluctantly gives in. “Let me just call my mom. I told her I’d only be over here for a little while.”

I make a face. “Why’d you tell her that?” It was unusual for our parents to care about how long we’d hang out with each other.

“I told you my mom wanted me home after school,” she reminds me.

“Yeah, but why?”

"Oh, um..." Lily takes a second to think before answering. "She just has a lot of chores for me to do today." She shrugs.

"Mkay," I respond. "Whatever."

Lily taps on her phone before bringing it up to her ear and waiting for her mom to pick up.

"Hey, Mom," she says into the phone. "Can I stay over at Tahlia's?"

There's a moment of silence as she listens to her mom's reply. Lily's face falls into a frown. Whatever her mom is saying, it can't be good.

"Yeah, I know," Lily groans into the phone, "but can't I get that all done tomorrow after the pool party?"

Another moment of silence. Another frown from Lily.

"Yes, I will! I'll still get it all done!" Lily protests.

I sit down on my bed and dangle my feet off the edge. This conversation does not sound like it's going the way I want it to.

"But, Mom," Lily starts again. "It's just that

this could be one of the *last* times—" She hesitates, looks up at me, and lowers her voice. "I just really think I can get it all done tomorrow."

I look up at her. What in the world is she talking about?

A smile crosses her face, and I know she's won the argument. Another win for her stubbornness.

"Yes, I promise," Lily eagerly assures her mom. "Okay, thanks, bye!"

She clicks off the phone and shoves it back into her pocket.

"Okay with your mom?" I stand from the bed with a hopeful smile.

"Good to go." She grins. "She said I could sleep over."

"Excellent." I rub my hands together like a maniacal villain.

"So, this plan of yours," she says, tilting her head to the side, and I instantly snap back into thinking about getting tampons from Sophie, completely forgetting to ask Lily what her mom was talking about on the phone.

"Genius, right?" I cock an eyebrow.

"It's not the *worst* plan I've ever heard," she admits.

"I'll take that as a compliment." I smirk.

"But what's going to happen when there isn't actually a ball in her yard?"

"I don't know. We'll just say it must've gone into a different yard or something. No biggie."

Lily chews on the inside of her cheek, giving her a pursed-lips expression. "All right," she says, giving in. "Let's go do this ridiculous plan of yours. But I state for the record that I think we should just ask your dad for money and walk back to the store."

A big, toothy grin spreads across my face.

"Quick, let's go before I change my mind," Lily adds.

Not needing to be told twice, I open my bedroom door, and we speed down the stairs. We march down my driveway and right back up Sophie's driveway.

Along with nearly every other house on the street, Sophie's house looks practically identical to my house, with the exception of an old basketball hoop above her garage door and an overgrown honeysuckle bush in her front yard.

When we were younger, Lily, Jackie, and I used to pick off the honeysuckle blooms and suck out the nectar, but I can't remember the last time we did that. It's probably been years, now. I can't even remember why we started doing it in the first place, but it sounds like something that would've been Jackie's idea. She used to enjoy coming up with weird things like that. We all did.

But now, the overgrown bush looks sad and forgotten.

Just as I'm about to stop at the bush and pick off one of the blooms, I feel a piece of toilet paper tickle the inside of my leg, so I march away from the bush and continue up Sophie's driveway.

When we get to her porch, I hesitate, for only a second, before knocking loudly on the front door. Willow instantly starts barking, and I hear someone trying to shush him. Footsteps pad over to the door.

The knob rattles, and the front door swings open, revealing the effortlessly cool Sophie. When she sees us, there is a flash of confusion on her face.

"Hi, guys," Sophie says as she uses a knee to block Willow from running outside. "What's up?"

"Hey, Sophie," I say, trying to make myself sound as cool as a cucumber and not like the fate of my future popularity rests in her hands. No pressure or anything. "We were just messing around with a soccer ball in my backyard and accidentally kicked it over into your yard. Could we come in and grab it?"

Sophie reaches down and grabs Willow by the collar so she can open the door wider without the dog running out. "Sure! Come on in."

I take a step inside and feel Lily follow me. Sophie shuts the door and lets go of Willow's collar. As soon as he is released, he's all wiggles, licks, and slobbers at the back of our knees. I give him a few scratches behind the ear. When Willow starts sniffing up the back of our legs, I take a quick hop-step forward, worried he might be a little too interested in the back of my pants. I've seen those Discovery Channel shows about wild dogs tracking down bloody animals. It's not pretty. The thought makes me shudder.

"The backyard is through here." Sophie motions for us to follow her across the living room and through a hallway to the back door. Her legs are tan and long.

I realize there's a slight possibility that someone might've seen us walk into her house and assume we're friends. That would be major. Being friends with Sophie would be even cooler than having Noah like me. The thought makes me smile.

Lily and I follow her with Willow at our heels.

My heart thuds in my chest. I know this is the part of the plan where I should be claiming that I need to go to the bathroom so I can snoop around. But as it turns out, my plan to flat out lie is a lot easier said than done.

When we step into the backyard, Sophie squints around, trying to spot the ball, and Lily narrows her eyes at me as if to say, *Get on with it!*

I puff up my chest.

"Actually, Sophie?" I say, mustering up all my courage.

Sophie stops scanning her yard and looks at me. "Mhmm?"

"I need to go to the bathroom." I scrunch up my face apologetically.

"Oh, okay! I'll help you look for your ball so you can get home quicker." She smiles, thinking she's being helpful.

My stomach drops. That was not the answer she was supposed to give. She was supposed to offer *her* bathroom for me to use.

I have to think of something fast.

"Uh, well, you see..." My eyes shift back and forth between Lily and Sophie.

We did not come all the way over here to leave empty-handed.

I bite my lip. "I kinda need to use it now. As in, *right* now." I do the little knee-bounce dance people do when they're really holding it. I'd rather let Sophie think I didn't know how to control my bladder than have her knowing I started my period.

Sophie's eyes go wide. "Oh! Right. Sure. There

is a bathroom first door on the right." She points back down the hall. "You okay?"

"Thanks! Yeah, no, I'm fine. Totally fine." I start walking backward toward the bathroom. "Just drank way too much water." I try to laugh, but it comes out like a snort. Internal face-palm.

Sophie gives me a curious look as she watches me retreat down the hall.

"Um, while she's in the bathroom, can I still look in your yard for the soccer ball?" I hear Lily ask Sophie as I spin away from them.

As I slip into the bathroom, Sophie replies, " 'Course! I'll help you look."

I lock the door behind me before swiveling to face the large mirror above the sink. The zit on my chin taunts me in its reflection.

I'm still here! Ha! Just because you forgot about me doesn't mean you got rid of me!

Curse my chin for allowing the pimple to grow and gain power! If I had more time in this bathroom, I'd try to pick at it again, but I'm on a much more important mission. The zit cannot distract me with its evil ways.

I look below the sink. There are four drawers of various sizes with small blue knobs.

If I were a tampon, where would I be?

I open the top drawer on the left. It holds nothing but unopened packages of toothbrushes and floss. The second drawer down is stuffed with clean hand towels. I have to shove them under the lip of the cabinet to get the drawer to close again. By the third drawer, which is filled only with extra rolls of toilet paper, my hands begin to sweat.

What if Sophie doesn't have any tampons and this whole plan is a bust?

Only one drawer left. I rub my hands together and pull it open.

And then I find it. The mother lode.

When I stare into the last drawer, I am greeted with the beautiful sight of two boxes of tampons, a large package of pads, and a stack of panty liners.

I let out a tiny squeal of joy.

My fingers pry open the tampon box and grab a few wrapped packages, which I shove into my back pocket. Hopefully, Sophie won't notice the new bulge at the back of my pants.

From outside the bathroom, I hear the back door open again, and Sophie and Lily's footsteps start back down the hallway toward me. Their voices echo into the bathroom. I grab two more tampons for good measure—I don't want another situation where I run out.

"Thanks for letting us look anyways." Lily's muffled voice bounces into the bathroom.

"No worries!" Sophie answers.

In case they can hear the water running from the hallway, I twist on the faucet and wash my hands. I don't want Sophie thinking I went to the bathroom without washing my hands. Then she might think I'm germ infested, which would not help my reputation one bit.

I shut off the faucet, dry my hands on a towel, and open the door.

Lily greets me with a pretend frown. "We couldn't find the ball in the yard. I think it must just be caught in the bushes along your fence or something."

I let out a pretend disappointed sigh. "Bummer."

Sophie smiles. "I hope you find it! And if not, I

think my sister may have an old soccer ball somewhere you guys can play with."

"Thanks, Sophie." I return her smile and try to position my body behind Lily's so that Sophie can't see that my back pocket has doubled in size.

"No worries!" She walks us back out into the living room and opens the front door for us to step out. When we do, she adds, "Tell your brothers I say hi!"

"Will do!"

I will certainly not be doing that.

We speed-walk down her driveway after Sophie shuts her front door. When we reach the sidewalk, Lily asks in a low voice, "Did you get any?"

I pat my back pocket and grin. "Mission accomplished."

CHAPTER EIGHT

Once we're back inside my house, Lily and I take the stairs two at a time up to my bedroom. As always, we quickly shut the door behind us. As soon as the knob clicks, I jam my hand into my pocket and pull out the stolen tampons.

No, not stolen. I prefer to think of them as *re-homed.*

Besides, I've always been a supporter of paying it forward—you know, where someone does something nice for you, and then you do something nice for someone else? Well, I've just now decided that one day when *I'm* sixteen and younger girls knock on *my* front door claiming to have lost a ball over the fence, I won't even bother looking for the ball. I'll just hand them the tampons right then and there.

So really, re-homing Sophie's tampons isn't *that* bad, because someday I'll pass along the favor. See? Paying it forward.

Unless...the younger girls really have lost their ball in my yard. Then there will be a very awkward moment when I hand them a stack of tampons and all they really want is their missing soccer ball.

"Why are they so small?" Lily asks, pulling me from my thoughts. She's staring at the little packages in my hand.

I look down at them too. I hadn't noticed it before, since I was so relieved to have found them, but they are very small—smaller than a lip-gloss tube.

"What in the world are these?" I hold up the wrapped things I swiped from Sophie's bathroom.

"Are you sure those are tampons and not those wipe things used for makeup?"

"I grabbed them out of a box labeled 'Tampons,'" I say, shrugging.

She squints at them. "But they are so tiny! The ones we got from the store were so much longer!"

"Maybe we should just unwrap one and take a look," I suggest.

Lily nods.

I pick at the plastic edges on one of the tampons until my fingernail slides under a fold and tears it open. The plastic wrapping falls to my feet, and I'm left holding something that looks like a cotton bullet.

"Huh?" My face scrunches up as I look at it. "Where's the rest of it? What am I supposed to do with only *this*?" I hold up the cotton specimen. "It doesn't even have the cardboard applicator!"

"I guess you just go in there and try to shove it up."

"Nice, Lily." I roll my eyes. "Way to get graphic."

She laughs.

"I'm being serious!" I playfully nudge her shoulder.

“So am I!” she says while still wearing a very unserious grin.

“Tahlia?” Dad calls from downstairs.

I hear his footsteps padding up the staircase.

In a moment of panic, I chuck the cotton bullet across my bedroom, and it hits the far wall with a thud before falling behind my desk, where it is safely hidden. Luckily, the others are still tucked away in my pocket, where they can’t be seen. Lily drops to the ground and sweeps the plastic wrapping under my bed. When we make eye contact, we both start giggling.

“Act normal!” I try to whisper to Lily between giggles.

“I’m trying!” she whispers back. “But why’d you have to throw it?” She chokes on a laugh.

This sets me off giggling again too. When I woke up this morning, I had no idea I was going to be hurling tampons away from Dad. What a strange day.

There’s a knock at my door. Lily and I both suck in a breath and whip our heads around to face the sound.

"You can come in!" I manage to squeak out, as I do my best to look relaxed and natural.

Dad pokes his head into the room. "Whatcha girls up to?"

"Nothing!" we say in unison. It sounds suspicious, and I know it, but if I say anything more to try to save our quick reply, it'll sound even more suspicious.

"*Okay* then," Dad says, raising an eyebrow. "Anyways, Tahlia, I was thinking we should go out to dinner tonight to celebrate your and your brothers' last day of school. Have anyplace in mind? Your brothers want pizza, but we just had Italian last night. Any other ideas?"

"Can Lily come?" I ask.

I'm not ready to be alone with just the men in my family and their weird testosterone. They won't understand what I'm dealing with. I need Lily there for support. Besides, we still haven't solved my tampon problem for Noah's pool party. So she can't leave.

"If Lily's parents are fine with it, then of course she can come," Dad says.

"My mom already said I could stay for the night," Lily assures him.

"Ah, I see. Well, then it's fine with me," he says. "The more the merrier."

"Cool. Then I want Mexican food," I declare. Lily and I both love Mexican food.

"Mexican it is." Dad gives a nod of approval. "I'll go tell the twins. Oh! And pack a jacket. It's meant to be chilly tonight."

He shuts the door behind him, and we immediately dissolve into giggles, which soon turn into full-fledged, hard-to-breathe belly laughs. When I'm finally able to catch my breath, I wipe my eyes and walk over to my desk to pick up the unwrapped tampon from the floor.

"I think it's safe to say I won't be figuring this tiny thing out anytime soon." I hold the bullet tampon out to inspect it. "It's way too small."

"Yeah, I don't think that's a starter tampon. That thing looks professional level."

"Girls!" Dad calls from downstairs. "Come on! Come down and jump in the car. The boys are hungry."

I roll my eyes to Lily. "Oh, well if the *boys* are hungry, we better hustle."

Lily hops up from my bed. "I'm hungry too. Let's go."

"Okay, okay," I say, and we make our way downstairs.

I hand Lily one of my jackets hanging on the rack by the garage door for her to borrow. Then I tug open the car door and climb into the far back seat. Lily scoots in beside me. Outside the car, Jamie and Ryan race each other to the front passenger seat, each pushing the other as they go. Ryan gets to the car first, but Jamie shoves him to the side. They struggle for the handle until Jamie gets the door open and sits down.

Lily chuckles. She thinks it's hilarious when they fight. I, obviously, do not. Mom once referred to their fights as "childish displays of dominance," which I thought was fantastic, because (a) anytime Jamie and Ryan are described as "childish" is a win in my book, and (b) it made them sound like they're part of the animal kingdom, which makes me laugh. Now I use the phrase whenever I can.

"Just get in the car and stop trying to *display your dominance*," I say to them.

Jamie reluctantly climbs into the middle row in front of Lily and me after losing the front seat to Ryan. "Oh, *whatever*, Professor Pee Pants," he shoots at me.

I gasp and give Lily an "I told you so" glance. She has to bite her lower lip to keep from giggling.

When Dad gets into the car, Ryan plugs his phone into the stereo, and we are forced to listen to his terrible music the entire drive. His music sounds exactly like how I imagine throwing pots and pans down a staircase would sound. Horrible. So it annoys me even more when Lily starts bobbing her head along with it. Whose side is she on anyway? If it were just Lily and me in the car with Dad, I know she'd want to listen to the pop playlist we made together on my phone.

By the time we park and walk into the Mexican restaurant, I'm already in a grumpy mood because of the music, but when we push open the door and step inside, my not-so-great mood completely drops to a terrible and absolutely *panicked* mood.

And *that's* because, across the room, Noah and his parents are sitting at the corner table with a direct line of sight to the entrance. At any second now, one of them will turn their head and see us standing by the hostess podium waiting to be seated.

Oh no. Please, no.

Usually, I'd want nothing more than for Noah to lock eyes with me in a Mexican restaurant, but I do not want that happening with my family around.

Ab-so-fruitly not.

My family will ruin any chance I have to ever make a good impression on Noah. I have no doubt Dad will accidentally bring up some humiliating story about me, thinking it's cute to share. And the terrible twins will *absolutely* do that—not even accidentally. They live to embarrass me.

Not to mention I still haven't dealt with the giant pimple taking up half my face. There is no way I can spend an entire meal with my hand slapped across my chin hiding it.

I need to stop this train wreck before it happens. Dad just cannot see Noah's parents and make me go over there.

"Uh, why don't we actually go next door to that pizza place like Jamie and Ryan wanted?" I say to Dad.

Lily can sense something is wrong, so she scans the room. When she notices Noah with his parents, she understands my desire to get the heck out.

"Yeah! I could go for pizza too!" she agrees.

We both nervously giggle.

"I thought you two wanted Mexican?" Dad raises an eyebrow.

"Dad, don't question their weirdness," Jamie grumbles. "Let's just go get pizza. That's what Ryan and I wanted in the first place."

"Yeah, Dad," Ryan chimes in.

"Yeah, Dad!" I add.

Dad groans. "Fine." He shrugs. "I guess I'm outvoted. Pizza it is."

I want to pump the air like I'm in some slow-mo sports movie, but I don't—knowing that'll only draw more attention to us. Can't risk Noah looking over and seeing us.

We turn to leave just as the hostess comes over with menus, ready to seat us.

"Welcome to Manuel's! Table for five?" she asks, motioning to the room behind her.

Dad shakes his head. "Sorry, not tonight actually. The kids have just had a change of heart on cuisine."

"Oh, no worries!" The hostess gives us a warm grin.

"We'll come back another night," Dad adds, as if the hostess's feelings were hurt by our leaving. "Anyways, thank—" He stops mid-sentence and points across the restaurant at where Noah and his family sit. "Look, it's the Campos family!"

Aaaand I've died on the spot. Dad just *had* to notice them, didn't he.

Lily shoots me a "well, we tried" look.

"We should go say hi," Dad says and starts walking over to where the Campos family is sitting. He works with Noah's mom every stupid day, but of course he needs to say hello to her now.

The twins mumble protests under their breath.

"Dad, we're hunnngry," they whine. And for once, I appreciate their complaints.

But it's too late. Dad keeps walking toward Noah and his parents. We're too far down the course of my personal nightmare, and there's no turning back now.

Ryan, Jamie, Lily, and I all drag our feet as we follow my Dad over to the far table where the Campos family sits. I just want Dad to say his quick hellos so we can walk away from their table. The longer my family is around Noah, the more chances they have to completely destroy my life. And if Noah thinks I'm uncool, then all my planning for tomorrow will have been for nothing.

As we get closer, I do my best to arrange my hair so that if I tilt my head slightly to the side, my chin pimple is covered. There's a good chance my neck will hurt if I keep it at this angle for very long, but it's worth it.

If there's truly no way to get out of this, I might as well plaster on a friendly smile.

"Hi, Rosa. Hi, Rob." Dad greets Noah's parents with a warm grin.

Noah's parents look up from their menus. When they see Dad, they grin.

Noah's mom, Rosa, has a wide smile, curly hair, and round-rimmed glasses. She looks like a person who'd dance to the jazz music in elevators, but I can't really explain exactly what about her makes me think that. I just have a pretty strong feeling that if I ever got on an elevator with Noah's mom, she'd start swinging her hips. I like her.

Noah's dad, Rob, has a bald head and a thick, square mustache. If I didn't already know that he worked at the flower shop on Carmichael Street, I'd probably guess that he was a firefighter or something. The only other person I've ever seen with a mustache like his was a fire captain from a television show Mom used to watch.

Popular people like Noah always have cool parents. It must run in the genes.

"Why, hey there, Grant!" Noah's parents say in unison to Dad.

Lily and I wave hello to Noah. If possible, he

looks even cooler than when we saw him earlier. He's put on a soccer hoodie, and his hair is messy.

"Hey, Noah," I say. My chin pimple better still be covered.

Noah smiles. "Hey, again. So random, right?" He pushes some of his messy hair off his forehead.

I assume he's talking about running into us again, so I agree, "Super random."

"Grant, these must be your sons. They look so much like you!" Noah's mom says, thankfully, saving me from having to explain to Dad what Noah's talking about. She motions to Ryan and Jamie, who both look bored out of their minds behind us. Luckily, when they realize they're being pulled into the conversation, they snap into their rarely seen polite versions of themselves.

"Nice to meet you," the twins say, turning on their charm.

"And *of course* we know these two lovely ladies, since they go to school with Noah," she says, grinning at Lily and me. "And you're coming to Noah's party tomorrow, yes?"

We nod.

"Can't wait!" I say with an uncomfortable laugh. I actually can wait. In fact, it would be *lovely* if Noah pushed the party to sometime after I've figured out how to use tampons.

"Going to be great!" says Lily, probably meaning it.

"Well, we just came over to say hello." Dad pats Noah's dad on the back as he motions around the room. "Don't want to intrude on your dinner." He taps his temple. "Great minds think alike on restaurant choices, eh? Especially when it comes to Manuel's Mexican food," Dad jokes.

I try not to audibly groan.

First off, Dad isn't funny. Why he continues to try to throw his hat into the comedian ring is beyond me. Second off, I've never understood the expression "Great minds think alike." Great minds do not think alike. Heck, for hundreds of years all the minds thinking alike thought the earth was flat, and they all turned out to be wrong. I could go on and on about that stupid phrase, but that's a rant for another time.

"We should throw a couple of tables together!" Noah's dad suggests. "Come join us."

My heart stops.

What did he say?! Join them?! Um, is it possible to hate someone you've just met? Throwing tables together sounds like a bad situation waiting to happen. My awkward dad and embarrassing brothers sitting next to Noah? Please, please, please, no.

"That's a great idea!" Dad declares.

"What about pizza?" Ryan softly moans.

"Not tonight," Dad curtly answers.

The twins and I know his tone all too well. It's his "I've had my final say, so don't argue" tone.

Mexican it is.

With Noah.

And Dad.

And my brothers.

Awesome.

At least I have Lily with me. She understands my pain.

Noah's dad beckons over a waiter, who helps us push another table up against theirs. I sit down between Noah and Lily. Across from me, Dad scoots a chair next to Noah's mom, and the twins grudgingly plop their butts down in the two remaining seats.

If this dinner is going to happen, I might as well make the best of it. I mean, hey, at least I get to sit next to Noah for the night. Maybe if I just drown out the sound of our parents' boring chit-chat, I can imagine we're actually close friends hanging out like normal.

Just a normal night with my friend Noah, yup.

"Did you two have a fun last day of school?" Noah's mom asks Lily and me once we've settled into our chairs. "Noah was at that after-school get-together, but I made him leave early to pick up some things from the store for his party tomorrow," she says, laughing. "He wasn't too pleased," she teases.

Noah rolls his eyes. "Mo-*om*."

A lump gets stuck in my throat.

After-school get-together?

Lily and I hadn't been invited to anything like

that. Noah and Jackie must've just left it when we saw them at the store.

I wonder who was there. Most of the class? No, no, couldn't be. They wouldn't invite Hannah Bean and not us. I mean, would they?

And who is *they*? Who threw this after-school get-together?

After tomorrow, more people will invite us to these types of things. Just another example of why tomorrow must be perfect.

"Yeah, we had a good last day," answers Lily.

I want to ask more about this *gathering*, when I feel someone come up beside me.

"Gooooood evening, everybody," says a waiter next to our table. "I've got drink orders in for this half of the table"—he points to Noah's family—"but can I get anything started for you guys?" He turns to face our side.

We all glance down at the laminated menus in front of us.

My neck is already starting to hurt from tilting my head to keep my hair covering my chin.

I wonder if when Jackie got picked up from school, she was going directly to the get-together.

"You guys should try the strawberry virgin margaritas," Noah says to Lily and me, snapping me from my thoughts.

I nearly choke on my own spit when he says the word *virgin*.

"It means it doesn't have alcohol," Lily mutters under her breath to me.

"Oh, right." I giggle uncomfortably.

"That's what I got," Noah continues. "It's really good. It almost tastes like a slushie or something." He leans back in his chair, cool and calm.

"Uhh," I rapidly flip to the drinks section of the menu so I can see what he's talking about. I want to take his recommendation, but I know I'm going to feel weird saying *virgin* in front of Dad.

"Just water for me," Dad answers the waiter.

The waiter nods.

"Can I have a Coke?" asks Ryan.

"Sure!" He scribbles down the order.

"Me too," Jamie agrees.

The waiter scribbles again.

I look up from the menu to see the waiter smiling down expectantly at me.

"I'll have the, uh, the strawberry virgin margarita," I manage to squeak. The awkwardness of saying the word *virgin* is made slightly better by the smile on Noah's face I see out of the corner of my eye.

"I'll have one too," adds Lily.

Under the table, I gently squeeze her leg in an attempt to thank her for not letting Noah and me be the only two to order something ridiculous-sounding.

"Oh! And here are some chips for the table!" The waiter holds out a basket, and I lean forward out of my seat to grab it. But when I sit back down and take a bite of one of the chips, Lily is looking at me with an uneasy and worried expression.

"What?" I ask her quietly.

She leans in close and whispers, "Um, well, don't freak out, but I think you bled through your pants."

CHAPTER NINE

My heart stops beating, and for a second I honestly think someone may need to perform CPR to bring me back to life.

Looks like I can never get up from this chair again. This is my life now. I'm here till my dying day. Bury me in the chair under this Mexican restaurant.

"But don't worry!" Lily adds quickly. "I was the only person who noticed. Everyone else's eyes were on the waiter."

Another lump forms in my throat. I try to

swallow it down, but it only sticks to the inside of my mouth like hot slime.

This is the worst thing to have ever happened to me in my entire life. I couldn't have just bled through my pants at home. Oh no—I had to bleed through in public, with my Dad and brothers, in front of Noah and his parents.

So much for making a good impression.

The embarrassment puke bubbles up again. I really think I'm going to be sick. If Noah sees my bled-through pants, I'm going to have to drop out of school, change my name, and move to Alaska. Maybe I'll take up dogsledding or moose herding and live in a tiny cabin so no one will ever notice if I bleed through my long underwear.

"What do I do?!" I half whisper, half choke to Lily. I can feel hot tears already starting to form at the rims of my eyes. They're just waiting for me to blink so they can run down my face and draw even more embarrassing attention to my awful situation.

"What are you two ladies whispering about over there?" Dad asks with a chuckle.

Everyone's eyes land on me.

That settles it. I'm putting Dad in a nursing home as soon as I get the chance. The man talks too much for his own good.

"How good the chips are!" Lily answers for both of us.

I let out a whoosh of air. Lily saves the day again.

"Well, don't keep it a secret," Dad says, laughing. "Pass the basket around!"

Without saying a word, I hand the basket to Noah, who happily pours a helping onto his plate. Can he hear me hyperventilating? I'm pretty sure everyone in this restaurant can hear me starting to hyperventilate.

"So, how's everything going in your department at work, Rosa?" Dad asks Noah's mom, and thankfully the adults are all drawn into his boring conversation.

I feel like I'm out of my body and watching the scene unfold from above. The adults chatter, the twins scroll through their phones, Lily stares at me with wide, worried eyes, and Noah happily munches on chips, probably thinking we're all having a good time.

Bless his popular little heart.

I have no idea what to do. My fingers dig into the bottom of my chair. I can't get up and go to the bathroom, because everyone will see the back of my pants as I walk off. But I also can't just sit here and bleed out more on this chair. I'm stuck with no options, and the longer I take to decide what to do, the worse the situation will become!

Noah leans forward in his chair. "So, did you guys get up to anything fun after we saw you at the grocery store?" he asks Lily and me.

I sneak a quick glance at Dad, who is thankfully still babbling on about work with Noah's parents and oblivious to our conversation.

"Oh, nothing." A.k.a. having a breakdown in the bathroom and sneaking into my neighbor's house. "Just, uh, hanging."

Just, uh, hanging? Get it together, Tahlia! That did not sound cool!

"I'm back with your drinks!" The waiter hovers over the table, carrying a large tray. He starts to set the drinks down on the table. When he places the large, fancy glasses with bloodred liquid in front of Lily and me, I think the world must be playing some cruel prank on me.

The drink is bloodred. Ugh. I mean, why wouldn't it be? Everything wants to taunt me today.

I gulp.

While the twins and Dad are distracted with the arrival of their drinks, Lily mutters to me quietly, "Tahlia, do you trust me?"

I frown. "Yes, obviously. Why?" I answer softly.

She makes a face. "Sorry about this."

"About wha—"

Before I even finish my sentence, Lily leans forward across the table and hastily grabs the basket of chips. As she pulls it toward her, her elbow knocks over my drink, causing it to topple across the table and completely pour out into my lap.

The cold drink jolts me back in my seat, and I let out a small yelp.

Ryan and Jamie instantly burst into laughter.

"What's wrong, *Professor*?" Jamie asks with a

chuckle. "I thought you'd be used to having wet pants."

The twins howl with laughter again. I could kill 'em, I really could.

I open my mouth, about to tell them to zip it, when Noah leaps up from his seat and grabs a stack of napkins from the end of the table.

"Here, take these!" Noah says as he thrusts them into my hand.

"Tahlia, I'm sooooo sorry!" Lily also stands from her seat and reaches for napkins to start dabbing the tablecloth.

The waiter, catching sight of the scene, rushes over with a roll of paper towels.

"Whoops!" he exclaims. "Accidents happen! No worries!"

Dad grabs the margarita glass and rights it, as Noah's parents scramble to stop the spread of the spilled drink farther across the table.

I look down at my lap with a horrified expression. My entire front is now completely covered in the sticky liquid.

It has stained my lap with its color.

Its *bloodred* color.

Suddenly, with great delight, I realize exactly what Lily has done.

With my lap covered in drink, no one will be able to tell the difference between the spilled margarita and my period! If I get up from the chair, they'll just assume it's from the spill!

My best friend is a certified genius.

"It's okay! It's okay!" I put up my hands.

The rest of the table is still busy mopping up liquid and fussing over grabbing more napkins for me.

"Really, I'm fine!" I say as Dad hands me napkin after napkin.

"I'll bring you another drink—free of charge," the waiter promises before hustling off.

Noah gives me a smile. "You okay?"

"Yes, um, totally good," I assure him. "Just a little sticky."

"Maybe we should go into the bathroom so you can dry off?" Lily suggests with a knowing smirk.

I try to hide my smile as I answer. It'd be weird if people knew I was actually pleased to be covered in margarita. "Yeah, let's." I turn to face the rest of the table and say, "We'll be right back."

As I stand from my seat, I hold my breath. It's the moment of truth. Once I turn and start walking to the bathroom, everyone will have a clear view of my bled-through pants. Hopefully, with the help of the virgin margarita, no one will be the wiser about what the stain really is.

I stand, turn, and wait for any horrified gasps or laughs from our table. But—to my great relief—they don't come. No one comments on the stain at the back of my pants.

Rejoice! Rejoice!

As I internally shout my hallelujahs, Lily and I make our way toward the restrooms, while diners at the other tables all stare sympathetically at the mess in my lap. No one in the entire place seems to be snickering, pointing, or whispering anything about periods under their breath.

I'm saved.

"That was amazing!" I exclaim as we step into the bathroom and the door swings shut behind us. I go to hug Lily, but she takes a quick step back.

"Yeah, yeah, I know I'm incredible, but you're still covered in sticky mess, so don't touch me," she says, scrunching her nose.

"All right, fine." I grin. Right now, I don't even care that my favorite jeans are ruined.

But as I look down my front, the excited rush I have been feeling sinks down to my toes. I was so happy no one saw my real stain, I almost forgot that I actually needed to come up with a plan for what to do next. I'm not out of the woods yet. And now I'm wet.

Lily pulls out several paper towels from the dispenser before running them under water from the sink.

"Here," she says as she hands me the dripping paper towels. "You should get that sticky drink out of your clothes before it dries and stains."

"Thanks," I say, taking them from her hand and beginning to dab my front.

"Do you think you bled through the pad or something? How did it get through to your pants?" Lily asks.

I scratch my nose, trying to work out what must've happened. "I guess so…"

Then the truth hits me like a cold slap across the face.

"No!" I gasp. "I actually forgot to put on a new pad before going to Sophie's house! All I have down there is folded-up toilet paper! No wonder it bled through!"

"Folded toilet paper?" She raises an eyebrow.

I frown. "Don't ask."

Lily shakes her head. "Well, just put on a new pad now, and you can tie this jacket around your waist to cover the stain," she suggests, holding out the borrowed jacket to me.

"But…" I chew my lip. "I didn't bring an extra pad to the restaurant."

"Why not?" Her eyes go wide, as if I've made a vital error.

I throw my arms up. "I got distracted and forgot!"

She puts her hands up to calm me. "Hey, don't get mad at me! I'm just trying to help!"

I give her an apologetic grimace. "Sorry."

"Just take a deep breath, okay? We'll think of something," Lily assures me.

The bathroom door swings open, and an elderly woman walks in. When she sees Lily and me standing by the sink, she eyes us curiously.

"You two in line?" the elderly woman asks, motioning to the bathroom stall.

"No!" we both reply as we step aside to let her pass. The woman shuffles into the stall before clicking it closed.

Lily and I exchange a glance. Since I don't want some random stranger overhearing us discussing my catastrophe, I change the subject as casually as I can to the first thing I think of—Mexican food.

"Uh, so, do you think you're going to get a fajita?" I ask Lily, stifling a nervous laugh.

Lily gives me a confused look.

I silently mouth, "I don't want *her*"—I point to

the stall the elderly lady is in—"to hear about…"—I point down to my pants.

Lily mouths back an understanding, "Ohhh," and clears her throat before answering. "I think I'm going to get the taco plate, actually. What about you?"

I stifle another giggle. The absurdity of us talking about Mexican food in the bathroom while I am covered in a virgin margarita and bleeding through my pants is not lost on me.

A small chuckle escapes from Lily. It's not lost on her either.

We stare at each with toothy grins, communicating through our expressions how funny this has suddenly become.

"I, uh"—I swallow my giggles—"I think I'll get a burrito." My cheeks hurt from holding in laughs, and I cover my mouth to keep from cracking up.

The woman in the stall must think we find Mexican food hilarious.

"That's a good choice," Lily says and grins.

The toilet inside the stall flushes, and the

woman pushes open the stall door. As she shuffles to the sink, she looks back and forth between Lily and me with a frown. We must look suspicious just standing around in the bathroom.

Not wanting the woman to alert the restaurant staff to our "suspicious behavior" in the restroom, I try to explain, "I spilled margarita in my lap." I point down to my front. "We're just cleaning it off." I flash the lady a wide, innocent grin.

"Aren't you a little young for a margarita?" She narrows her eyes and looks me up and down.

"Sorry! No, I meant *virgin*. We're virgins," I quickly correct myself with a chuckle.

Lily whips her head around to me. Her eyes bulge out of her head as she gives me a "What did you just say?" stare.

The woman's mouth drops open.

When I finally realize what has just come out of my mouth, I'm horrified.

"I mean the drink! The *drink* was virgin!" I sputter.

But it's too late. The woman has already marched

out of the bathroom with a frown plastered across her face. When the door swings shut behind her, Lily bursts out laughing.

"That went well!" she manages to say between laughs.

I shoot her a look. "Oh, shut up. That did not go well at all! What if she goes and tells the waiter we're in here and—"

Lily waves a hand in my face. "Tahlia."

I continue, "—the waiter thinks we're doing something bad and—"

"Oh, Tahliaaa."

"—they come in here and realize I bled through my pants and—"

"Tahlia!" Lily points at something over my shoulder.

"What?"

Lily puts her hands on my shoulders and spins me around to face the bathroom wall.

"Do you see what I see?" she asks.

I raise an eyebrow. I don't see anything out of the ordinary. "A tiled bathroom wall and a paper-towel dispenser?"

"No, to the left of the paper-towel dispenser." She tilts me slightly.

I squint. There, just to the left of the metal box of paper towels, is another metal box attached to the wall. I've seen it in loads of bathrooms before, but I've never actually paid any attention to what it is.

I step forward to see the writing on its label.

In thick, boxy, black letters, it reads, **MENSTRUAL PRODUCT DISPENSER**.

If it wasn't a cold metal box on a public bathroom wall, I'd give it a big ol' squeeze. It's the most beautiful thing I've ever laid my eyes on.

The right side of the metal box is labeled **PADS**, and the left side is labeled **AMPONS** (because the letter **T** has been scratched off).

I let out a huff of breath in relief. "Great spot, Lily." I squeeze her shoulder. "Thanks!"

"Don't thank me yet," she says, still looking at the metal box.

I follow her eyes. She's staring at a small sticker in the right-hand corner of the box that reads, **ALL PRODUCTS 75¢. QUARTERS ONLY.**

"Do you have any quarters?" I ask hopefully.

Lily shakes her head. "No, I don't. I don't have any money on me at all," she says, shoving her hands into her pockets and turning them inside out.

I snap my fingers. "The money from my grandma! Do you remember what we did with the change from the grocery store?"

Lily bites her lip. "Uh, you specifically told the cashier to 'keep the change,' if you remember."

Unfortunately, that did ring a bell.

I frown, wishing I could go back to that moment and pocket the money instead.

"Why does this keep getting more and more complicated?" I groan. "Why did my period have to come today?!" I drop my face into my hands, willing myself not to cry in a Mexican restaurant bathroom. Everything that could have gone wrong today, has.

"I'm sticky, I'm stained, and I still have the biggest zit on my face." My words come out between ragged breaths, and a sob-lump forms in my throat. "I shouldn't even go to the party tomorrow. It'll just make everything worse."

Lily rubs my back, and I have to look up at the ceiling to keep tears from streaming down my cheeks.

"This sucks. It really does," she says calmly, "but we can't stay in this bathroom forever. Let's just try to come up with a plan, okay? Maybe you could just stuff your underwear with more toilet paper?"

I make a face and hold back tears. "I will if that's my *only* option, but I'm worried that if I only use toilet paper again, I'll bleed through even more." I slip off my jacket and hold it up. "And if I tie this around my waist, I could, you know, bleed through my jacket too!" My voice breaks on the word *jacket* as I struggle to keep the sob-lump from coming out.

Lily continues to rub circles on my back. I feel pathetic and I know I look pathetic. Why is it that when boys go through puberty, they just get all oily and sweaty for a few years, but when *girls* go through puberty, Madame Maturity cackles a maniacal laugh and makes sure *everything* is terrible?

Lily snaps her fingers. “I’ve got an idea!”

I look up at her and wipe my nose. “You do?”

“Yes! There’s a fountain outside!”

“Okay, and...?” I cross my arms, not following.

“And you know what people throw into fountains?” she prompts with a wide grin.

It takes me a moment to catch up with what she’s saying. When I finally realize what she’s getting at, I bounce up and down. “Coins!” I answer.

“Exactly!” She beams and rubs her hands together. “Coins! Let’s go fishing in the fountain for some quarters!”

CHAPTER TEN

The fountain outside Manuel's Mexican restaurant is one of those weird ones with little chubby cherubs spitting water out of their mouths. I have no idea who thought water-vomiting babies were appropriate for Pennsylvania strip-mall fountains, but there are some things in life that are best not to question.

The only problem is, the fountain is located directly outside Manuel's front entrance, and I 100 percent do not want Dad, my brothers, or Noah seeing Lily and me leaving the restaurant to take quarters from it. We'll look like we're stealing.

Well, I guess, technically we will be stealing. But it's for a good cause!

"How are we going to get through the restaurant and to the fountain without my dad noticing?" I ask Lily. "I'm pretty sure if he sees us leaving the restaurant, he'll have some serious questions."

Lily taps her chin. "We'll just have to sneak behind the other tables and get out the front door fast."

"Because *that* won't look suspicious," I say, rolling my eyes.

"Have any other ideas?" she shoots.

If I were an action hero, this is where I'd do a backflip out of the bathroom window, race down the alley next to the restaurant, dive into the fountain, and grab the quarters—all without ever being noticed. However, since I can't even reach the bathroom window on tiptoe, the bathroom door is our only viable exit.

In order to get outside to the fountain, we have

to go back through the dining room. There's just no way around it.

"No. I don't," I admit. "We'll do your sneaking-behind-the-tables plan."

Lily shakes her head. "I don't want it to be *my* plan. I'm just saying it is *a* plan."

"Too late. It's *your* plan. Which means you get to walk out first." I nudge her to the door.

"Fine," she grumbles. "But first let's scope out a good path through the restaurant away from your dad."

"Good idea."

We poke our heads out of the bathroom door and survey the restaurant. I hunker down in a crouching position, and Lily hovers over me.

Manuel's has about fifteen tables total that are occupied by a mixture of families, groups of friends, and couples. Our table is to the right of the bathroom door. Our front-door exit is no more than twenty-five steps in front of us. Luckily, Dad and my brothers are facing the opposite wall. They'd have to turn in order to see us sneaking out.

Unfortunately, Noah and his family are facing

the middle of the room, so if we're not careful, they could easily look up and see us racing out to the fountain.

"Is anyone from our table looking over here?" I ask. "I can't tell." From my angle, I can barely see the faces of the Campos family through all the table legs and human legs.

"No, it looks like the waiter is taking their orders," Lily whispers.

"Ugh. I really hope Dad makes sure to say 'no onions' in whatever he orders for me."

Someone walks by the bathroom door, so we pull our heads back inside.

Lily says, "I'm going to sneak behind the tables that are to the left of the bathroom. Then I'll make a beeline for the exit."

"Sounds good to me."

"And we're just getting the quarters and coming right back, yes?" Lily confirms.

"Correct," I agree.

"Are you ready?" she asks.

"Ready," I say. "I'll be right behind you."

Without a second glance back, Lily steps out of

the bathroom and crouch-walks toward the closest table to the left of the bathroom door.

While her crouching method may be the best in making sure anyone from our table doesn't spot her, she does get several curious stares from people who see her in the low position. But it's too late to tell her. All I can do is go out after her.

She kneels down behind a table and pretends to tie her shoes while she waits for me to catch up. I push out the bathroom door and follow her path to the left-hand-side tables. All we have to do now is walk the twenty-five steps to the door without being spotted.

I realize too late that I've still got the red, sticky mess down my front. It's not helping me blend in at all. The wet paper towels really didn't do much of anything except add to the dampness of my jeans and shirt, so by the time I reach Lily behind the table, most everyone on this side of the restaurant is staring at me with curious expressions.

I'm really doing a horrible job at not drawing attention to myself.

"I say we just make a dash for it," Lily says when I kneel down next to her.

"Agreed." I nod.

"On the count of three?"

"Yes."

"One—two—"

"What are you two girls up to?" a voice barks from above us before we can get to three.

We look up from our crouched positions behind the table and see the elderly woman from the bathroom standing next to the table and glaring down at us.

"Why are you hiding next to my table?" She crosses her arms. "Where are your parents?" She swivels her head around the restaurant.

Lily mutters, "Oh, no, we were just—"

"I—uh, I thought I dropped something over here," I say with a soft chuckle, hoping she believes the tiny white lie.

The woman glares at us and waggles a finger. "You two are up to something. I know it."

"We aren't!" Lily and I say in unison. We really

need to stop answering questions at the same time. It's extremely suspicious.

"I've got my eye on you two," the woman warns as she takes her seat at the table. "You better not try to swipe my purse off the back of my chair. I'll alert the staff," she huffs.

I let out a little whimper.

"No, we aren't—" I begin to protest, not wanting the woman to think we're troublemakers. But before I can finish my sentence, Lily pushes me forward.

"Just go!" she says. "No one at our table is looking!"

At her command, I speed-walk toward the restaurant's front door, leaving the elderly woman frowning and clutching her purse.

The closer we get to the hostess podium, the faster my heart thumps in my chest. From this angle, Noah could look up at any moment and see us leaving the restaurant. I can only imagine how weird that conversation would go.

Oh, Mr. Wilkins?

Yes?

Your daughter appears to be running away from dinner.

She's what?!

Yeah, I'm sure Dad would take that *real* well.

I give my table a side-eye glance to make sure I'm still in the clear. Luckily, I am. My brothers are still scrolling through their phones, Dad and Noah's parents are deep in conversation (probably something snooze-worthy), and Noah is sipping his virgin margarita, oblivious to his cuteness.

Sigh.

Lily joins me at my side.

"Keep going!" she whispers. "We're almost there."

Together we take the final steps past the hostess podium and push through the door to step out onto the sidewalk. The fountain looms ahead, with its water-vomiting angel-babies and all.

We jog over to it and both lean over the fountain's edge to peer at the coins under the water.

"See any quarters?" I ask as I squint into the fountain.

"Not yet. Just pennies and nickels. You?"

“Same. And one dime.”

“Wait, I see one!” Lily exclaims.

“Where?”

“There!” She points to the middle of the fountain, and then I see it too.

It’s clearly a quarter, because it’s much bigger than the surrounding coins. The only issue is, it’s too far away for me to simply reach over and grab it out of the water. It is practically at the center of the fountain.

“And there’s another one right next to it!” Lily points out the second one.

“But we can’t reach them from here,” I groan.

Lily looks down at my jeans, then back up at me. “Looks like you’ve got to roll up your pants and get in.”

I moan. “I was worried you were going to say that.” I take a deep, long breath. “Maybe we should just think of something else. I’m not sure getting into a fountain is the best idea.”

Lily crosses her arms. “Tahlia, come on. Just get in. I told you before we left your house that I was hungry. Now I’m starving. Do it so we can go back to the food. I bet it's at the table by now," she says, practically salivating.

"Well, *sorry* if I think figuring out my bled-through-pants situation is a bit more important than your taco plate," I shoot.

Since Mom is gone, Lily is the only person I have to help me. I don't want to come second to her Mexican food. Lily should be completely on my side and not try to rush me.

She narrows her eyes at me. "Are you honestly suggesting I don't think it's important? After I went to the store *and* Sophie's with you? And then after—"

"Okay, okay. Fine. I know you think it's important." I wave her off, not wanting to get into an argument. "I'll go in the stupid fountain," I say.

"And go fast!" she adds. "We don't have much time. We said we were only going into the bathroom to dry you off. I'm sure they're starting to wonder where we are."

"I'm going, I'm going," I say, already slipping off my shoes and rolling up my pants. These jeans have been through a lot today.

Poor pants.

Once my cuffs are rolled, I scoot my butt to the edge of the fountain before dipping my toes in.

"It's cold!" I whine.

"Do you want a pad or not?" Lily raises an eyebrow. "If you don't want to put folded-up toilet paper in your underwear, you've got to get in that water and find those quarters."

I look over my shoulders to make sure no one from school is about to see me knee-deep in a fountain. If they do, well, I guess I still have my move-to-Alaska plan.

"This is miserable," I huff as I fully submerge my feet. The water reaches to the top of my calves. Once my feet are used to the cold water, I wade through the fountain toward the closer of the two quarters.

Did I start this day thinking I'd be covered in period, virgin margarita, and fountain water? Nope. No, I did not.

"Keep an eye out for a third quarter too," I say to Lily over the sound of the cherubs spitting water.

"I am." She leans forward to get a better look at the coins.

The first quarter shimmers under the water below me. I reach down, pick it up, and drop it into my pocket. Then I wade toward the second quarter.

I'm just about to bend down to pick it up when a loud cough comes from behind me.

"Ahem!"

My heart stops. I know Lily's cough, and that's *not* Lily's cough.

Startled, I whip around, only to see the scowling face of the elderly woman from the restaurant. Lily takes a few steps back from the fountain and gives me a "this can't be good" expression.

I know how bad the situation must look. I'm in the middle of a public fountain picking out coins after sneaking through a restaurant where the elderly woman thinks I drank an alcoholic beverage and possibly stole purses. Can't say I blame her for thinking we're up to no good.

The woman clears her throat again and raises an eyebrow.

I'm frozen, unsure what to do.

The woman glares at me.

I stare at her.

"I—I can explain," I stammer, giving in to her death stare.

"I think you better," she retorts, putting her hands on her hips.

"Well, you see," Lily says, trying to help, "we were just . . ." She trails off, unsure how to explain what we're doing.

Lily and I exchange another glance. There's nothing we can say that would make this scene come off any better.

Nothing to see here! I was just wading in a cold fountain for fun!

I don't think so.

The woman's lips settle into a deep frown. "You were just what? Stealing? Should I call your parents?"

Yeah, this isn't going well.

If this woman goes back into the restaurant and tells Dad what I'm doing now, I'll be grounded for life. Plus, I'm pretty sure that'd ruin my chances of Noah thinking I'm cool. I doubt I'll be invited to sit with the popular crowd once he learns I'm a small-time criminal who pockets coins from a strip-mall fountain.

"Well?" The woman taps her foot.

The embarrassment puke bubbles up into my mouth again, and I know there is really only one thing I can say that could possibly save me from a lifetime of being grounded in my bedroom. And as much as I don't want to, I close my eyes, take a deep breath, and begin the explanation that I hope will stop her from going in and ratting us out to Dad and the police.

"Well, I..." My voice sticks in my throat. I cough to unstick my words. "I'm in the fountain because..."

The woman doesn't stop tapping her foot. "I'm waiting."

I close my eyes and try again. "I'm in the fountain because I got my period and bled through my pants, but I don't have a pad, so we're trying to get three quarters so we can get some products from the dispenser in the bathroom without my dad knowing." The words tumble out of my mouth faster than I intend.

Lily gasps so loudly, her jaw practically hits the ground. I'd gasp at myself if I could.

The woman blinks at me.

There's a pause before anyone speaks.

"I see," the woman finally says, with her lips pursed and her hands still on her hips.

My heart thuds in my chest. I can tell by the way she's looking at me that I never should have told my secret to this stranger.

The woman is about to stomp back into the restaurant and tell on us—I just know it. She'll pivot on her heel, march up to Dad, and demand that I'm properly punished for thieving. All for three stupid quarters!

To my surprise, she doesn't turn from her spot. Instead, her frown fades, and she unclasps her purse to rummage around inside. It only makes my heart beat faster.

"When I got my first period, I had to learn how to use a sanitary belt," the elderly woman says, still digging through her purse. "I bet you girls don't even know what that is." She chuckles.

Lily shakes her head no. I try to shake my head, but I can't move. I'm frozen in place just like the fountain cherubs as my period confession plays over and over again in my head.

"I'd say you're lucky, but *I* never had to go fountain diving for coins back when I still had mine, so I think we're even on unfortunate period stories," the woman says and chuckles again.

I'm not sure how to respond. My legs can only tremble.

She's no longer frowning, which seems like a good thing, but her face is hard to read. For all I know, she's digging through her purse for her police badge so she can arrest us for swimming in a public fountain. If this goes on my permanent record, I'll have to plead on my knees for mercy from the judge.

It's my period, Your Honor! She's the true guilty party! Let me walk free!

"Here," the woman says while pulling something out of her purse and holding it out for me.

My legs are still shaking, but I slowly waddle over to her—still worried it's all just a trick to get me close so that she can put me in handcuffs.

When I reach the side of the fountain, I hold out my hand to her, and I'm speechless when she drops three quarters into my open palm. I wrap my fingers around the coins. They're probably the best thing I've ever been given in my entire life, and I want to wrap my arms around the woman but don't think she'd appreciate sticky virgin margarita and cold fountain water down her front.

"I don't have any pads to give you, but hopefully these will help. Next time just remember to bring extra products with you so you don't have to steal from public fountains."

I quickly nod.

"And put that quarter back," she instructs, pointing at my pocket.

I do. Immediately. I pull the fountain quarter out of my pocket and drop it into the water so fast, you'd think it had been burning a hole through my jeans.

"Thank you," I say to her, still in disbelief. "Thank you so much. I..." I trail off. I want to properly thank her, but I'm not sure what to say. How do you properly thank someone for period quarters while you stand in a fountain covered in virgin margarita?

She shrugs and gives me a knowing smile. "Anyone who has ever had a period has a few less-than-pleasant stories to tell. Glad I could help get you through yours."

I stare at the coins in my hand, feeling tears starting to form in my eyes again. If I blink, they'll run down my face.

"We, uh, better get back inside," Lily says, motioning toward the Mexican restaurant. I know she's worried about how long we've been away from the table and eager to get some food, and I'm thankful for the distraction from my possible crying.

"Thank you again," I say to the elderly woman as I step out of the fountain and roll down my pants over my wet calves.

"You're welcome," she says. She smiles before patting my shoulder and turning to walk away.

Lily tugs on my arm. "Let's go," she says.

After I step back into my shoes, we dash back toward the restaurant door but pause before pushing it open.

"Should we just make a run for the bathroom?" I suggest, not wanting to be seen by Dad as we come back in. That's just as suspicious as going *out*.

"Might as well," she says. "Our crouching didn't really work that well anyways. The only reason they didn't see us was due to dumb luck."

"Agreed."

"What if someone from our table sees us running back through the restaurant to the bathroom? What do we say then?"

I chew my lip, thinking. "I don't know. We'll just make something up. We can just say we forgot something in the bathroom and we're hustling back to get it."

"Good plan."

"Ready?"

"Ready."

We push open the door. The smiling hostess picks up menus, ready to greet us, but when she sees my red, sticky front and my wet jeans, her face drops.

The hostess points to my pants. "Umm, you're dripping wet—" she starts, but we don't stop to hear the rest of her sentence. We race straight past her and all the way back into the bathroom.

As soon as the door closes behind us, Lily points to the product dispenser and asks, "Pad or tampon?"

Not wanting to be in another unusable-tampon situation, I say, "Better play it safe with a pad. I can't waste time or quarters messing up my chances with a tampon."

"Good point."

I stuff the quarters into the machine as fast as my fingers will let me. When all three quarters are in, I spin the dial until it clicks, and a small white box falls out of the machine and into my open hand.

As much as I'd like to do a victory spin around the bathroom, I don't have time for a happy dance. Surely our entire table must be already wondering why it's taken us about twenty minutes to clean up a spilled virgin margarita.

After rushing into the bathroom stall and sticking the new pad to the inside of my underwear, I tie my jacket around my waist so that no one will be able to see the original stain. I've never felt more like a mature woman and a diapered baby at the same time. It's an odd combination.

With my pad and my jacket securely in place, I finally march with Lily out of the bathroom and back to our dinner table. Dad sees us walking over and greets us with a grin.

"There you girls are! We were starting to worry you got sucked into a bathroom portal or something!" He laughs.

I sigh. There he goes again, trying to be funny.

"Just lots of spilled drink to clean," I say, pointing to my red lap. I hope they don't realize that I've barely cleaned it at all and that my front still looks like it did when we left for the bathroom.

He nods. "Well, we went ahead and ordered for you. Got you both burritos. Hope that's okay."

"With no onions, right?" I confirm. After

twelve years of my pushing onions off my plate, Dad should know to never order them for me.

"Whoops—I thought you liked *extra* onions." He chuckles at his own joke. "I told the waiter to put in as many onions as he could!"

I don't bother to acknowledge the nonexistent humor. This is his strange way to confirm that he got my order correct.

"Thanks, Dad," I say as I take my seat next to Noah.

"You all good?" Noah asks once Lily and I have settled back down.

"Totally." I smile.

"Next time I'll suggest a less-sticky drink, in case it ends up down your front," he says.

My stomach does a flip.

He said, "Next time."

Next time!

As in, he pictures us having dinner *again*. Maybe Lily and I will be invited to hang out with the cool crowd!

I try not to bounce up and down in my chair.

Lily, who must've overheard Noah's comment,

gives my leg an excited little squeeze under the table.

For the rest of the dinner, I fantasize about all the "next time" dinners Noah and I might possibly have. By the time the adults pay the bill, I've all but completely pushed the fountain misadventure from my thoughts.

CHAPTER ELEVEN

I'm still covered in the red, gross, margarita mess on the car ride home from the restaurant. Even though I'm almost dry, the seat belt sticks to my shirt, and my brothers don't miss a beat in making fun of me the entire journey.

I try to ignore them. See what I have to deal with? What I'd give for them to be shipped off to boarding school.

As soon as we get home, I change into my pajamas, toss the stained clothing into the hamper, and hand Lily my blue pajama set for her to borrow for the night.

"Want to watch a movie?" I ask once we're both dressed for bed.

"Always," Lily says.

We race down the stairs to the living room and flop onto the couch. I grab the remote and start flipping through our saved movies. When an interesting-looking romantic comedy flashes across the screen, I click on it.

"Have you seen this one?" I ask.

Lily makes a gagging sound. "Looks stupid."

She's right, of course. It *does* look stupid, but I love romantic comedies. I can't help it. Who wouldn't want to be at the center of a rom-com and always feeling special?

I continue to scroll. "What about this one?" I say as I click on a new superhero movie.

"Nah." She makes a face. "Not in the mood for superheroes," she says, yawning.

I continue to scroll.

"What about *Jurassic Park*?" Lily suggests once we've scrolled past most of the movies.

I cross my arms across my chest and give her an annoyed look. "Why do you always want to watch that old movie?" I sigh.

"Dinosaurs are cool." She pokes my side. "Remember when we used to dig in your backyard looking for fossils and bones?"

I roll my eyes. "That was, like, five years ago."

"Not even! *Three* years," she says as she leans back into the couch. "Anyways, I can only watch those types of movies here. My parents don't let me watch scary stuff."

"That's one of the benefits of older brothers," I say, nodding. "My parents gave up trying to stop me from watching what the twins get to watch. Your new baby sibling will also get those benefits." I chuckle. "They'll get to watch whatever you watch."

"Oh, right. Sibling benefits." Lily picks at her nails. "Tahlia, I've been meaning to tell you—"

Suddenly, Ryan hops over the back of the couch and slides into the cushion next to me.

"You guys are watching *Jurassic Park*?" he asks.

"Great movie," Jamie adds as he swings his legs over the couch next to Ryan.

"Shut up. Lily was talking," I say, then turn back to Lily. "Yes?"

She eyes my brothers and brings her knees up to her chest. "Never mind. It's nothing."

I raise an eyebrow. "You sure? Didn't sound like nothing."

There's a sinking feeling in my stomach that she's about to tell me something bad. I try to shake the feeling.

She quickly nods. "Yeah, it was nothing—let's just watch *Jurassic Park*."

I narrow my eyes at her, aware that she's changing the subject. It's not like her not to tell me things.

"She said it's nothing. Let's watch the movie," Jamie whines.

"No," I groan. "Can we watch any movie other than that one?"

"Looks to me like you're outvoted," Ryan says, wrestling the remote from my grip and scrolling through the options, looking for the stupid dinosaur movie.

Lily perks up in her seat.

“You realize this will be, like, the fifteenth time we’ve watched this, right? I think I could say it word for word at this point.” I make a face at Lily.

“You should be proud,” she says, smirking. “Besides, you owe me for today.”

“Why does she owe you?” Ryan asks.

“No reason,” I quickly say. “Just start the movie.”

I shoot Lily a glare. She grins back.

“Quiet—it’s starting,” Jamie shushes us.

I sink back into the couch and settle into a comfortable position. Once Ryan has the remote, there’s no chance I’ll ever get it back. Besides, who knows? Maybe the sixteenth time seeing the movie will really blow me away. Not.

For the next two hours, we watch the movie, and I try not to think about what Lily was about to tell me. Luckily, after a while, I’m engrossed in the stupid dino movie and no longer thinking about whatever she wanted to say.

As much as I wish I didn’t, I still jump at the scary scenes, gasp at the near deaths, and sigh when it seems like everything is going to turn out all right at the end. But that doesn't mean I actually *like* the movie, okay? I still maintain that sixteen times is fifteen times too many to watch dinosaurs. Weren't we supposed to outgrow liking dinosaurs and digging for fossils in elementary school?

In the last ten minutes of the movie, I hear a sniffle to my left. I sneak a quick glance at Lily. Her eyes have a watery film, and it looks like she's holding back tears. She sniffles again, and I look back to the screen, since I don't think she'd want me calling attention to her crying with my brothers here. They'd just make fun of her for liking the movie too much. Which, clearly, she does. I mean, I *know* she likes this movie, but I've never seen her cry over it before.

As the credits roll, Ryan and Jamie lazily stretch and slowly stand from their seats. Jamie gives me a swat on the back of the head before saying, " 'Night. I'm going up to my room."

"Me too," Ryan agrees. "Later, Professor. 'Night, Lily."

I reach for one of the decorative pillows to chuck at him. "Don't call me that!"

He dodges it easily and chuckles as he follows Jamie up the stairs.

"They're so dumb," I mutter under my breath. I expect Lily to say something about the movie or my stupid brothers, so when she doesn't, I look over at her.

She's silently rubbing her eyes.

"Are... are you okay?" I ask quietly.

She doesn't look up as she wipes her nose. "Mhmm," she says, nodding.

Her reply does not convince me that she's okay.

"You sure?"

She nods again.

"You must really like that movie if you're still sad when it ends, eh?" I joke, trying to lighten the mood.

Lily doesn't respond, and for a moment I think I've hurt her feelings. Right when I lean forward to apologize for the joke, she wipes her nose and gives me a weak smile.

I smile back. "Lily, if something is wrong, you know you can tell me—"

"I said I'm *fine*," Lily snaps, completely throwing me off guard. She wipes at her nose again.

I suck in a breath. We don't normally fight, but this feels like it could be turning into one, and I'm not even sure why. What did I do?

Since I'm not exactly sure what to say, I decide to play it safe and apologize. Only, I'm not exactly sure what for.

"I, uh, I didn't mean to—" I start.

"Do you wanna get some ice cream?" she asks, cutting me off. Maybe she isn't upset? Who knows—she usually isn't like this.

"Oh, um, sure." I narrow my eyes at her. "You're really okay? Do you want to tell me what you were going to say?"

Lily ignores my question. "Ice cream. Come on." She stands up from the couch.

I follow her lead and stand up from the couch.

We stroll into the kitchen and help ourselves to huge scoops of mint chocolate chip. I make sure Lily's is extra big. A little extra ice cream always makes people feel better.

By the time our bowls are licked clean and our

sweet teeth are satisfied, Lily no longer seems sad. She just seems tired. We both lean back in our kitchen chairs and let our sleepiness take over. Our eyes droop and our arms sag by our sides.

I let my mind wander to tomorrow's big day.

Noah's party is only twelve hours away, and I still haven't figured out how to use a tampon or how I'm going to be able to get in the pool. I haven't solved any of today's problems. I've only created new ones. But I'm too sleepy to come up with any more ideas. Guess my period pool problems will have to wait for the morning.

I yawn.

"Come on," I sigh as I rise from the chair. "Let's head up to my room."

Lily also yawns. She grunts as she stands from the chair and follows me to the sink to drop in her bowl before we drag ourselves to my bedroom.

I want to ask her again about before, but the words don't come out. If she's mad at me for something, I don't want to make it worse by prying. And truthfully, the last thing I want is a fight the night before the pool party.

Lily climbs into the left side of my bed, which is closest to the window, and tugs the covers high to her chest. I switch off the light before blindly feeling my way into the right side of the bed, which is closest to the door.

The left side of the bed will always be Lily's, and the right side will always be mine. At this point, it'd probably be weird to switch bed sides. Jackie used to sleep in the middle, but there's more room in the bed without her, so it's much better.

The only thing I miss about sleepovers with Jackie is the back-massage trains we used to have. Lily, Jackie, and me—all lined up. It's hard to have a massage train with only two people.

But, no. This is better. Much better. Now I'm not all cramped on the edge of the bed.

I stretch out my legs and blink until my eyes adjust to the dark. When they do, I stare up at the ceiling. There are still a few glow-in-the-dark stars left over on my walls from when I plastered my room with them when I was eight. I really should get around to peeling them off so it doesn't look like a kid's room anymore. That's what the new and improved Tahlia would do. Maybe I'll even give my whole room a makeover. Something that says, "This room belongs to a *sophisticated* eighth grader."

"What a day," I sigh.

I can feel Lily's pillow move beside me, so I assume she's nodding. It's hard to really see her with the only light coming from the glow-in-the-dark stars.

There's a beat of silence, and I think for a moment she's drifting off to sleep, but then she flips onto her side to look at me.

"Hey, Tahlia?" she says.

I flip onto my side too, to face her. Our noses are inches apart. "Yeah?" I whisper.

"Who would you have called today if you hadn't called me?" Lily asks.

I draw my eyebrows together. "You mean, like, to come over and help me with my period?"

"Mhmm, yeah." She nods. "Like, who do you think is cool in our grade? If I wasn't able to come over, who would you have called?"

I prop my head up with my elbow. "Well, those

are very different questions. I think Noah and his friends are cool, but I never, *ever*, not in a million years, would've called them about my period." I make a disgusted face.

Even though it's dark in my room, I can see the whites of her eyes when she rolls them. "No, not cool like *that*. I mean people who are cool in a friend way."

I chew the inside of my cheek. Her questions make me uneasy.

"Why?"

The comforter moves up and down with her shrug. "I don't know. Just curious, I guess," she sighs. "If this had happened last year, you could've called Jackie."

A hot pulse runs down my spine. I don't want to think about Jackie. It makes me too annoyed.

I try to keep my breath steady and calm, since I don't want Lily to hear how fast my heart is beating now that I'm thinking about how close we used to be with Jackie.

"Well, yeah. We were friends with Jackie last

year. Now we're not," I say, trying not to grit my teeth.

"I know." Lily flips onto her back with a huff. "But I think..." She pauses. "I think you—we—*could* be friends with her again."

"What are you talking about?" I ask, very confused. "I don't want to be friends with her again."

"You don't?"

"No!" I scoff. "She's all"—I pull my hands out from under the covers and wave them above me—"well, you know what she's like."

Lily uses her elbow to prop up her head. She studies me.

"What?" I ask. "You really think I want to be friends with *her*?" I narrow my eyes at Lily, suspicious. "If this is about the party..."

She shakes her head. "Huh? No. It's not." Lily flops back onto the pillow.

"Then what?"

"Never mind."

"You can't act all weird and then say 'never mind.'"

She blows a strand of hair away from her face. "I just wanted to know who you would have called if I hadn't been able to come over today. We don't really hang out with anyone else anymore."

If my plan goes well tomorrow, maybe we will.

But I don't say that out loud. I don't want Lily to think I'm trying to replace her or anything. I just think it would be nice for at least a couple more people to think we're cool.

So instead, I pinch her shoulder and say, "*You're* my best friend."

"Yeah," she says. "And you're my best friend."

We both look up at the ceiling and let silence fall between us again. I want to ask her more about why she brought up Jackie, but I don't. I'm nervous that I won't like her answer. Does she want a different friend or something?

I'll ask her about it in the morning when we're not both so tired. Maybe she will want to talk about it then.

Lily breaks the silence again. "So, Noah's party tomorrow," she begins. I can practically hear the smirk on her lips. "Are you still excited?"

"Obviously!" I squeal with a giggle.

We both laugh, and I'm happy for the conversation switch.

I scrunch my nose. "I'd be more excited if I could figure out this whole tampon thing before then, but that's looking pretty unlikely at this point."

Lily taps her chin, thinking. "Hmm, we could fill the entire pool with strawberry margaritas so no one will be able to tell you got your period!"

We giggle even harder, and I pull the blanket higher to my chin.

I'm not exactly sure when, but after a few more minutes of talking with Lily, my eyes begin to droop. It's only when I blink my eyes open again that I realize she's already fallen asleep.

I roll over and check the time on my phone. It's nearly 4 AM—a lot later (or earlier, considering it's now technically the morning) than I thought. I must've fallen asleep too.

I roll back over. Lily has sprawled out in the night and taken over most of my bed, leaving me a dingy corner, just like Jackie always did.

Typical.

I shove her back over to her side. She doesn't wake.

Something in my underwear feels wet, and I almost start to panic, thinking I've peed the bed. My head starts spinning with bed-wetting nightmares, and I'm about to throw back the covers in horror right as the period events of yesterday come rushing back into my memory, and I realize it's probably just my new, uninvited period guest. I might need to change the pad.

Not wanting to ruin my sheets, I slowly swing my legs over the side of the bed and tiptoe over to grab one of Mom's pads that I stuffed into the back of my desk. Sure, it's the middle of the night, but I may as well change it now before I have another bleed-out situation.

When I step into the hallway, it's quiet and dark. There's no light coming out from under Ryan's or Jamie's doors, so I let out a sigh of relief. Usually in the summer they stay up way too late playing video games, and I don't want them to try to use the bathroom while I'm in there.

The tile flooring of the bathroom is cold, so I do a quick little hop-step to the toilet so my toes don't touch the ground. I yawn as I plop down on the even colder toilet seat. With half-closed eyes, I rip off the used pad from my underwear and tuck it into the trash before tearing open the new pad. Just as I'm about to stick it to my underwear, something catches my eye.

There, right behind the bathroom door, is a tampon tucked into the corner. Lily must've slipped it under the door yesterday and I missed picking it up. Since she slipped so many tampons under the door, it probably got lost in the shuffle and rolled next to the wall.

I stare at it.

It stares at me.

With a grunt I reach over and pick the tampon off the floor and roll it between my fingers, examining it.

"I can figure you out," I whisper to it.

It doesn't say anything back because, well, it's a tampon.

I continue to roll it between my fingers as I listen for any movement outside the bathroom door. It's still silent.

Lily, my brothers, and Dad are all asleep.

I decide that the middle of the night is as good a time as any to give tampons another go.

With determination, I peel back the plastic on the tampon and chuck the wrapper into the trash. I take a deep breath, lean forward, and try putting it in.

And it . . . *goes in.*

It just slides right in!

The inner tube pushes perfectly into the outer tube and there is no splash from inside the toilet bowl. I wiggle around on the seat to make sure it's not uncomfortable, and I don't feel a thing!

I've done it.

I've actually, really done it!

Who knows if I'll ever be able to do it again, but who cares? I'm pool-ready! I've mastered tampons!

If it weren't four in the morning, I'd let out a victory whoop. But since I don't want to wake my brothers, I wash my hands before tiptoeing quietly back into my bedroom.

Lily is sprawled out across the bed again. In fact, without me under the covers, I think she's taken up even more space.

"Lily!" I shake her awake. "Lily, wake up!"

Her eyes are still closed when she groans, "What?"

"I did it!"

"Did what?" she mumbles. "What time is it?"

"I used a tampon!"

She smacks her lips in that tired way people do when they're just waking up.

"Huh?" She flips to her side, clearly not understanding how important this moment truly is.

I shake her again. "I *said*, 'I used a *tampon*!' "

Lily yawns and blinks her eyes open. "You used a tampon?" she repeats.

"Yes!"

"How? Wha—when?" she stammers and starts to sit up, finally catching on.

"Just now! In the bathroom!" I bounce up and down on the bed. "I went in to change my pad and found a tampon on the floor. I tried giving it a go, and it worked."

A smile forms on her lips when she finally realizes what I'm saying. "Yes!" She gives a tired fist pump.

"Yes!" I mimic her fist pump.

Lily folds back the covers on my side and pats the mattress. "Now get back in bed," she mumbles. "I was having a good dream. What time is it anyway?"

I tap my phone on the nightstand. It lights up and reads 4:23 AM.

"It's four in the morn—" I look back at Lily and realize she's already drifted back to sleep.

Ah, well. We can celebrate more tomorrow.

I climb into bed beside her and fall back asleep while thinking about how fantastic Noah's pool party is going to be now that I'm a bona fide tampon user.

What could go wrong now?

CHAPTER TWELVE

It's hot and stuffy in my bedroom when I wake up. Somehow, I've managed to wrestle all the heavy covers from Lily, who is now curled into a little ball on the edge of the bed. No wonder I'm sweating. I kick the covers down to the bottom of the bed and stretch my arms above my head.

Lily always sleeps in later than I do. Most of the time I'll mess around on my computer until she wakes up, but today is no ordinary day. Today is Noah's pool-party day. And I'm too excited to patiently wait.

I tap my phone. It's 8:10 AM—a perfectly reasonable hour to wake someone up.

"Lilyyy," I coo as I walk my fingers up her arm. "Wakey-wakey. Noah's party is less than two hours away!"

Lily stirs and slowly opens one eye.

"Morning," she answers with a groggy voice.

"Good morning!" I say back in a singsong voice.

"How did the tampon work out overnight?" She rubs her eyes.

I suck in a sharp breath. I'd almost forgotten about my triumphant tampon victory!

In one swift movement, I jump off the bed and run my palm along my sheets, checking for any signs of leakage. The blanket is dry and clean (well, except for the blue nail polish stain from when I knocked over the tiny glass bottle months ago).

I twist around to get a good look at the back of my pajamas. They look totally normal and dry too. No bleed-through at all!

"I think it worked!" I squeal.

Lily climbs out of bed and spins me around to double-check the back of my pajamas.

"Yup, no bleed-through," she confirms.

I race to the mirror over my dresser and lean in close to check my chin. To my great surprise, the pimple has miraculously shriveled up overnight. All that's left is a tiny, barely noticeable red dot. Yes!

I clap my hands together. "This is going to be a good day. I can feel it."

"And you can go swimming now that you have a tampon in!" Lily exclaims.

"That's the plan," I say, nodding enthusiastically.

"Will you need to change it before the party? I think you only have those weird, unusable bullet-tampons left," she says, frowning.

I wrinkle my nose. "The instructions we read yesterday said I should change it every eight hours."

"Or when needed," Lily adds.

"How am I supposed to know if it's needed?"

"You're asking the wrong gal." She shrugs.

“Well, I put it in around four in the morning, so four plus eight hours is . . .”—I count on my fingers—“around noon. So I should be okay, since the party starts at ten.”

“Oh yeah, you’re totally fine,” Lily agrees. “You can keep it in.”

I do a little happy dance. “I think this calls for a celebration breakfast. Complete with cinnamon rolls and scrambled eggs.”

Lily groans, “I need to go home to get my swimsuit and stuff ready for the party.”

I make a face. “Okeydoke. Well, I’ll tell my dad we need to swing by your place to pick you up on the way. That way we can still arrive at the party together. I want to make sure nothing ruins this day.”

“Oh,” Lily looks down at her hands. “I’m not sure . . .” She trails off.

“About what?”

She shrugs. “Maybe it would be easier to just meet at the party?”

I can’t read her expression. She glances away from me and starts pulling her hair into a bun.

“Why would that be easier? Wouldn’t it be better to just take one car? Besides, I want to get there at the same time as you so we can walk in together. I don’t want to arrive alone.”

Lily rubs her arm and shifts her weight. “I think my mom wants to drive me.”

“Okay.” I shrug. “Then I’ll just walk over to your house and come with you in your car.”

There’s a beat.

“On second thought,” she says and chuckles, “you’re right. It’ll be easier for you to just swing by and pick me up.”

I raise a questioning eyebrow. She’s acting weird again.

“You sure?”

“Definitely.”

“All right,” I say, unconvinced. “Whatever works.” I narrow my eyes at her.

There’s another beat of silence between us as I wait for her to say something more. It feels like I’m missing something obvious, but I can’t put my finger on it. This would be a good time for me to ask more about why she was acting weird last night, but at the same time, I don't exactly want to poke the bear so close to Noah's party.

I decide to ask her more after the party. I'll make her tell me why she was crying and why she brought up Jackie.

"I should get going," she finally says. "Can I wear your pj's home?"

"Duh. Besides, I know where you live. I can always hunt you down if you don't return them," I say, cracking a smile. I'm not even sure why she's asking. She wears my clothes home all the time.

Lily gives me a weird half smile as she nods. "I'll text you when I'm ready to go?"

"Works for me."

"Sweet. See you in a bit." Lily tucks her phone into the waistband of my pajamas.

"Later!" I say.

She gives me a quick wave before opening up my bedroom door and padding down the stairs. I hear the front door open and close as she leaves.

I tap my phone again. It's 8:16 AM.

I officially have one hour and forty-four

minutes to get ready for what could be the most important party I'll ever go to. Whatever I choose to wear now might be an outfit I remember for eternity, so I can't just throw on any ol' thing. It has to be perfect.

Just as I slide open my closet, there's a knock on my bedroom door. Assuming it's Lily and she's just forgotten something, I say, "Come on in!"

My face falls when I see it's not Lily but my brothers. They poke their heads into my room.

"What do *you* guys want?" I sigh.

With a smirk, Ryan pulls a soccer ball out from behind his back. "Sophie just brought this over for you and said she was sorry you couldn't find *your* ball. She said that her sister doesn't use this one anymore, so you can keep it."

My eyes go wide with horror. *See?* This is why I didn't trust Sophie. I knew she would tell my brothers I went over to her house.

"You don't have any soccer balls. What was she talking about?" Jamie presses.

Oh no, oh no, oh no. How do I explain this?!

I mean, I *guess* it is kinda nice of Sophie to send

the ball over, but now I have to continue my dumb "lost my soccer ball over the fence" lie.

"Are you, like, into sports now?" Jamie continues to taunt as he steps into my room.

"Maybe," I snap as I grab the ball out of Ryan's hands.

"Then show us a move or two with that ball, you Olympian," Ryan cackles, following Jamie in.

Great. Now I'm going to have to take up soccer, all just to cover up the real reason we went to Sophie's house.

I groan and try to push them back out the door. It doesn't work—they are like brick walls.

"Come on—get out. I'm busy," I whine.

They don't listen. Jamie plops down on the edge of my bed, and Ryan grabs the soccer ball out of my hands. They start to throw it back and forth over my head.

"No! Guys! Get out!" I moan again.

My phone vibrates on my side table, and I lunge for it before Jamie or Ryan can grab it first. When

I look at the screen, Mom's picture flashes, so I hit Accept as fast as humanly possible.

"Mom?!" I practically gasp into the phone.

"Hi, sweetheart," Mom answers. "I finally have some time and service to call you back from yesterday. What were you trying to tell me?"

I glance up at my brothers. They're still tossing the ball back and forth like five-year-olds. Seriously, you would never guess these guys are sixteen.

I pull the phone away from my face and snap at my brothers, "Can you please get out?"

My brothers need to leave my room for me to properly explain to Mom everything that happened to me yesterday. I can't talk about my period woes with them here.

But of course they ignore me. They continue to toss the ball back and forth.

"Guys!" I snap again.

They pretend not to hear me whine.

"Tahlia, can you hear me?" Mom's voice echoes out from the phone.

I bring it back to my ear. "Yes, I can!" I shout.

"Okay, well, I only have a few seconds before I have to get on the road. Just wanted to check in real quick to make sure you're doing all right. Everything okay?"

"Yeah, I—" I look up again at my brothers. There's no way I'm going into the details of yesterday with them listening. I guess I *could* run outside to speak with her in private, but that'd mean leaving my brothers in my room alone. Last time they were in here alone they changed all the settings on my laptop. It took me weeks to get everything back to normal.

Even though that was before I added passwords onto all my devices, I still do not want them alone in my room snooping around. They might find Mom's pads stuffed in my desk.

Jamie tosses the ball to my feet, and I flinch on instinct. "Aw! Come on, soccer star!" Jamie laughs.

"Yeah, we just want to see your skills!" Ryan adds.

"What's going on, Tahlia?" Mom asks, pulling me back to the phone.

"Jamie and Ryan won't leave my room," I whine

to Mom as Ryan grabs the soccer ball back off the floor.

"We're leaving, we're leaving," they moan. Now that they've been ratted out to Mom, they move a lot quicker to my bedroom door.

"Honey?" Mom says.

"Yeah, one second, Mom," I huff as I push my brothers out and shut my door behind them.

"Oh, shoot. Sorry, hon, I have to actually run. Jan is calling me," Mom says.

"No, but I can talk now!" I blurt. "The boys are gone!"

"We'll talk tonight when I get home, okay?" Her voice already sounds distant, like she is pulling the phone away from her face.

"Wait!"

But it's too late. Jan (whoever she is) has weaseled her way into what was meant to be my conversation. Ugh!

I toss my phone back onto my bed.

Whatever. Maybe I don't need Mom anyways. I figured out how to use a tampon without her, my pimple is gone, and Noah's party is going to be great. No one will ever need to know about the day Lily and I had yesterday. Yesterday can be just a bad memory I never talk about again.

I spin away from my bed and march toward my closet. My clothes are messily stuffed into cubbies or hanging inside out. There are a few dresses on the floor that seem to have fallen off their hangers, and I kick them to the back so the closet door doesn't run over and rip them.

The clothes I haven't worn in a while are folded in three rows on the shelves. I reach for my pair of flowery shorts near the bottom of the stack. As I pull them out, the whole row topples over, making even more clothes pile up on the floor. I don't bother to pick them up.

I step into my bathing suit before pulling on the shorts, since I don't want to waste precious time at the party having to change. Then I try on the shorts, a pair of pants, two dresses, and a romper Grandma Judy bought me last Christmas that is still too big. Finally, I settle for an old pair of jean cutoffs, because nothing else seems right. To finish the look, I tug on a blue V-neck shirt and slide on my flip-flops.

And *voilà*!

I tap my phone for a third time. It's 9:02 AM.

T-minus fifty-eight minutes until the party. I've gotta get moving if we're going to get there on time. I've never understood why adults always want to be "fashionably late." Isn't it bad to be late? When I'm late to class, I get detention.

I open my bedroom door and hustle to the top of the stairs.

"Dad!" I call down the steps.

"Come down here if you want to talk to me!" he shouts from somewhere on the first floor.

Typical. Absolutely typical. My parents yell for me all the time when *they* are in different rooms! I would get in such big trouble for yelling back, *Come here if you want to talk to me!* to them.

I groan and race down to find him. He's sitting at the kitchen table eating a bowl of cereal while reading one of his dull business magazines and wearing his pajamas. When I walk in, he doesn't look up.

"Dad," I say again.

"Mornin', Tahlia," he says as munches on the cereal, still reading.

"We have to stop to pick up Lily on the way over to Noah's party," I state.

"Pick up Lily to go where?" He puts down the magazine.

I shoot eye lasers at him. "Noah's party. Remember? It's today. You said you'd drive me."

"Oh, right," he says, nodding. "Maybe Ryan or Jamie could drive you so they can get some driving practice."

"What!?" I moan. "No! You said you'd drive!"

My pulse picks up speed. The very last thing I want is for my brothers to have an opportunity to ruin my party entrance.

"Okay, okay," he says, waving me off. "Let me get dressed." He stands up from the table, magazine still in hand.

"But hurry, because we have to pick up Lily on the way."

"What time does the party start?"

"Ten."

He rolls his eyes. "Tahlia, we've got loads of time. The Camposes' house is not that far."

"Yeah, but—"

"And eat some breakfast before we go," Dad says as he walks out of the kitchen.

I look over at the box of cereal on the counter. I hate to admit it, but he does make a good point. My stomach is grumbling, so I grab the box and pour some into a bowl.

I wolf it down quickly, wanting to be ready to go as soon as Dad is dressed. But after the cereal's gone, I only end up impatiently waiting for the next twenty minutes. My foot taps our wood floor.

When Dad finally does reappear, I swear I've aged twenty years.

"Let's go!" I whine. Lily hasn't texted me to say that she's ready yet, but I'm too excited to wait.

Dad follows me into the garage and into the car. Then we back out of the driveway and drive around the corner to Lily's house. Before the car rolls to a stop in front of her house, I'm already flinging open the car door.

"Tahlia!" Dad grumbles. "Don't open the door while the car is moving!"

I ignore him as I race to Lily's front door and give it a good thump. There are rustling noises from inside, and I can hear Lily shout to her parents, "I'll get it! I'll get it!"

Lily opens the door a tiny crack and pokes her head out. I try to peer inside, but she uses her body to block my view into her house.

"Um, hi?" I say, confused by her awkward stance. Usually she opens the door wide to let me come in.

"Hey, Tahlia. Let me just go grab my bag and I'll be right back in a second," she huffs breathlessly. She must've run to the door.

I take a step closer, ready to follow her inside to her room.

"I'll really just be two seconds." She closes the cracked door a tad more. "You, uh, you can just wait here."

I try to look behind her. "Did you get a dog or

something that you don't want to let out? Why are you keeping the door closed like that?"

"A dog? Oh, no." She gives a quick laugh. "I, uh, I'm just making sure to keep the AC in the house."

"It's not even that hot out," I say and look up at the sky. Maybe she knows something that I don't about a heat wave coming. More heat would be good for Noah's pool party.

"Yeah, I know, but it could get hotter later in the day," she says, shrugging.

I raise an eyebrow. "You really want me to just wait out here?" I point to where I'm standing on her front porch. "You don't want me to come in?"

"Honestly, I'll be right back!" she says while closing the door, not even really answering my question.

I cross my arms and try to look in the window next to Lily's front door, but unfortunately, the blinds have been pulled down. Just when I'm about to walk around to look in the kitchen window, Lily slips back out her front door, carrying her bag and towel.

"Ready!" she says cheerfully. "And I've packed

sunscreen"—she pats her bag—"in case you need to borrow some."

I bite my lip, remembering I'll need it for my legs now that I'm not wearing board shorts. "Whoops, yeah, I did forget mine," I admit.

"I've got you covered," she says and grins before skipping down her front lawn to the car.

I stay on her porch a moment longer, hoping to catch a glimpse inside her house. Something is off. I just can't tell what. Does it have something to do with the new baby?

As we climb into the car, Dad is staring at Lily's house.

"I'm sure you've got lots of good memories there," Dad says to Lily as she tugs on her seat belt.

Lily's eyes go wide. "Yeah, um, yes." She nods.

I give Dad a weird look. What a strange thing for him to say. He must be in a sentimental mood. He gets like this some days. Next thing I know, he'll start talking about how fast we're growing up.

"Dad, just drive!" I roll my eyes.

The closer we get to Noah's house, the more eager I become. My right leg bounces up and down and up and down like a nervous twitch, and I can't stop grinning.

Dad turns the car down a street that begins to look familiar from last year, so I know we're getting close to Noah's house. Not wanting another situation like last night at the restaurant, where Noah has to endure more time with my family, I point to a corner up ahead and say, "Dad, you can just drop us off here."

"Nice try, Tahlia," he scoffs. "I'm not dropping you guys off on a random corner. I'm taking you all the way to the house." He puts up a hand. "And don't worry, I won't go inside and embarrass you in front of all your friends or anything."

"Fine," I groan as I slump back in the seat.

Dad pulls the car up next to the curb outside Noah's house. It looks nearly identical to every other house on this street and yet, even though this is only the second time I'm seeing it, I'd be able to pick it out instantly.

It has two stories and a small porch with a white swing. The concrete driveway is cracked in a squiggly line, and there is a tree in the front yard with lots of wide branches that look great for climbing.

Lily, Jackie, and I used to find the *best* climbing trees in the park behind our middle school. I wonder if Noah used to climb this tree.

"Have fun!" Dad twists in his seat to face us.

"You can go now," I say over my shoulder as I climb out of the car.

"I'm going to wait until you two get to the door," he says, pointing to Noah's house.

I roll my eyes. "Whatever."

My flip-flops squeak as we race from the car to the doorstep. Lily reaches out and presses the doorbell, and I turn to give Dad the "Get moving!" wave. He gives me a salute before driving off.

We wait in silence on the doorstep. After a few seconds, I nervously start picking at the hem of my blue shirt. It does look nice with my jean cutoffs, but maybe I should've gone with my yellow dress instead of this casual shirt. The dress is more of a party outfit, right? Or are dresses too babyish?

Ugh. I wish I could change. Stupid blue shirt.

The doorknob jiggles and I let go of my shirt and smooth my hair down, wanting to make a good impression on Noah as soon as he opens the door.

I hear footsteps inside the house and take a deep breath. This is it. This is my moment to shine.

CHAPTER THIRTEEN

When the front door swings open, it's not Noah. It's Noah's mom smiling down at us. I try to hide my disappointment.

"Hi, girls! Fun dinner last night!" Noah's mom grins. "Glad to see you all cleaned up and dry, Tahlia," she says, chuckling.

The door opens wider, and Noah steps out from behind his mom. His hair is wet, and he's wearing blue swimming trunks with little green palm trees on them.

"Thanks for getting the door, Mom. You can go

back upstairs with Dad now," he says in between breaths. He sounds as though he's just sprinted across the entire house.

"Oh, right!" His mom winks at Lily and me. "I know the deal. We parents are so *embarrassing*." She makes a face like she's sharing some inside joke with us. "You know how it is."

Lily and I chuckle so that we don't seem rude.

"I'll see you two later," Noah's mom says to us before disappearing into the back of the house.

Noah gestures for us to come inside. "The party is out back. Come in!"

We follow him into the house and look around. It's just how I remember it. Inside is airy and bright. Family photos hang on the walls, and a blue couch takes up most of the living room.

Through a large sliding-glass door and a wall of windows on the opposite side of the house is the huge backyard, with a basketball hoop at one end and an old tree house at the other. Smack-dab in the middle of the yard is the pool, complete with a waterfall and slide.

Three of our classmates are already in the

pool—Rebecca Jordan, a girl with black hair who always wears the coolest earrings; Harrison Lopez, a kid with freckles who *swears* his parents let him go bungee jumping while on vacation (he has no proof); and Dean Bighman, the tallest kid in our grade, whose real name is Albert but who started going by his middle name at the beginning of seventh grade.

Their voices and laughter echo into the house.

Noah leads us toward the backyard. I step over the wet footprints that he must've made by racing from the pool to the front door. He slides open the glass door, and we hear music blasting from large speakers hanging on a huge wooden awning.

Once we step outside, I can see a few more of our classmates hanging out around the pool.

I try not to frown when I see Jackie climbing up the ladder to the slide. Her long hair is pulled up into a high ponytail at the top of her head, and she's wearing a black bikini that actually makes her look like she has boobs.

A bubble of jealousy forms in my chest. My swimsuit does not give *me* any boobs.

"Lily and Tahlia are here!" Noah calls to our classmates.

They all turn and wave, probably expecting me to be wearing some embarrassing outfit. I smugly grin when they see I'm not wearing board shorts this year.

"There are sodas and drinks in there," Noah says, pointing to a large cooler. "And snacks there." He points to a table covered with chips, cookies, and various other sweets. "We ordered pizza for lunch, so that should be here in an hour or so. And you remember where the bathroom is if you want to change into your suits."

"I've actually already got mine on under my clothes," I say, pleased with my genius planning skills. Now I won't have to waste any time away from the party while changing.

"Me too," says Lily.

"Awesome," Noah says. "Then, yeah, just set down your stuff wherever and jump in."

"Do a flip, Noah!" Amir Abdi, the kid who loves jamming pencils up his nose, calls from a pool chair.

Noah takes a running start before flipping into the pool. When his head pops back out of the water, he gestures for Lily and me to jump in too.

Lily mutters under her breath so only I can hear, "Are you still, uh, *secure* down there?"

"Should be," I whisper back. "It hasn't been in for eight hours yet."

"Come on!" Noah slaps the water. "Jump! Jump!"

The rest of the group joins in. "Jump! Jump! Jump!"

I kick off my flip-flops and pull off the clothes over my bathing suit. Lily does the same.

It's the moment of truth. If the tampon doesn't work when I hit the water, and blood swirls out into the pool, I'll have to pack up and leave town.

I hesitate before taking a step closer to the pool's edge.

"Together?" Lily reaches for my hand.

"On the count of three." I take her hand in mine. "One . . . two . . . three!"

We leap into the pool to the cheers and whistles of our classmates. As soon as my head pops above the surface, I do a quick scan of the water to make sure there is no red anywhere.

Luckily, there isn't. There's no red to be seen.

No leaks! I've perfected swimming on my period! I am the Tampon Goddess, and pads bow before me!

Suddenly, I'm hit with a blast of water. My hair falls into my eyes, and I spit the chlorine taste from my mouth. When I turn to face the culprit, Noah is smiling with his hands above the water and ready to splash again.

"Hey!" I laugh and send an even bigger splash his way.

It turns into a full-on splash war. Lily and the rest of the group in the pool join in. After I send a particularly large wave of water crashing down on Noah, he sputters and puts his hands up in defeat.

"Okay! Okay!" he says, laughing. "You win."

I stick my tongue out at him. He wouldn't playfully splash someone he didn't like, would he?

My heart skips a beat. I think my plan is working.

"We should play Marco Polo!" Dean suggests.

"Oh my gosh. I think I stopped playing that game when I was six," Jackie says, rolling her eyes.

I want to remind her that we played Marco Polo two years ago in her aunt's pool, but I don't.

"Know any other pool games, Jackie?" he shoots back.

She taps her chin. "What about...Truth or Dare?" She smiles.

Lily and I exchange a glance. We've played Truth or Dare before, but never with *boys*. What if I'm dared to kiss someone or say something really embarrassing?

When Lily and I play, we always pick truth, then ask each other the same lame questions, like *What's your favorite color? Who is your favorite teacher? Have you ever cheated on homework?*

"Nah, let's have chicken fights instead," Noah says.

I let out a sigh of relief.

"Does everyone know how to play?" he asks the group.

"*I* know what chicken fights are," Jackie announces. "It's where two people climb on the shoulders of two other people in the pool, and then they try to knock each other over. If you stay up, you win!"

"Yeah, exactly," Noah says, nodding.

"I'll go first!" Jackie raises her hand. "Amir, let me climb on your shoulders."

Amir bends down in the water, allowing Jackie to scramble up his back. When she's sitting on top of his shoulders, he stands and roars, "No one dares to challenge us! We can't be beat! We are the best!" He splashes the water, and Jackie covers her eyes with a scowl.

"Noah should go, since he suggested the game," Lily pipes up. "And Tahlia, why don't you be his partner?" she adds.

I shoot her a look. What is she doing?

She smiles and shrugs.

"For sure!" Noah exclaims. "Come on, Tahls. Climb up." He sinks lower into the pool.

I cover my mouth to hide my grin.

Tahls!

He's given me a nickname! Surely that means he thinks I'm cool.

Encouraged by how well my plan is going, I swim over to him in order to climb up onto his shoulders, but just as I'm about to hop on, my mouth goes dry and my heartbeat quickens.

Periods and chicken fights probably mix as well as elephants and glass doors. Not at all.

I take a step back from Noah. "Actually, I don't know. Maybe Lily should go."

I can't ruin how well this party is going. If my tampon string were to come out in the middle of the game with everyone watching, I think I'd actually die.

Noah spins around to look at me. "What? No, you'll be great!"

"Yeah, come on, Tahlia!" Jackie taunts playfully.

Not able to think of any decent excuses as to why I can't compete, I reluctantly climb up on Noah's shoulders. My heart thumps in my chest.

Please, Madame Puberty, let the tampon stay in place. Take my soul, but leave my tampon string.

When I'm up on his shoulders, Noah stands tall and makes his way closer to Amir.

"I'll be the ref!" Dean calls. His voice breaks on the word *ref*, and he turns a bit red.

No one says anything about the voice crack, but we all heard it.

Probably trying to move past the awkward moment, Dean quickly adds, "Whoever falls back into the pool first, loses."

Noah and Amir line up across from each other. Jackie gives me her best "game on" face.

Dean raises his hand in the air. "Ready, set, chicken fight!" He slaps the water.

Jackie and I both put our hands out in front of us as the boys rush at each other. I try to focus all my attention on the fact that Jackie looks like a crazed animal ready to knock me into the water, and not on the fact that if I'm jostled too hard, my tampon string might pop out of my bathing suit.

When we're finally close enough, Jackie's arms collide with mine, and we both splay out our fingers as we wrestle with our hands. I can't read her expression. She has this strangely enthusiastic and determined look, like she's excited to make me fall. Or maybe she's genuinely happy and concentrating on the game. Whatever it is, it makes me want to win even more.

I jerk her right, but she balances out. She jerks me left, but I stay up. Noah takes a half step to the side to keep us straight, and Jackie laughs as we struggle to remain upright.

So that's how she's going to play it—laughing at me in front of everyone. Laughing like she doesn't care at all about my feelings. It feels like she wants to see me humiliated.

I won't let her win. No.

I grit my teeth and try pulling her forward, but she leans back and nearly tugs me along with her. Our audience oohs, aahs, and cheers.

I give a quick side glance to the water below me to make sure there is nothing red dripping into it, just as Jackie wraps her arms around mine in an attempt to push me backward.

Noah wobbles below me. I grab ahold of Jackie's hand just as she begins to fail to keep her balance. Her failing tips me forward, and we both topple into the pool, sending water spilling over the top of the pool edge.

When we come up for air, I adjust my bathing suit—and thankfully, everything is still in place.

"Tahlia and Noah win! Jackie hit the water first!" Dean announces.

I beam.

Jackie laughs and wipes hair out of her eyes. "Wow. You're strong, Tahlia," she commends with a smile.

For a second, I'm caught off guard by her comment. I can't tell if she's actually complimenting me or if she's being sarcastic.

Even though I'm still unsure, I smile. And there's a brief moment of old familiarity between Jackie and me. It's weird, but nice.

"My turn!" Rebecca says, splashing into the pool between us.

"I'll get on your shoulders, Bec," Harrison jokes.

"I bet I can take you!" Noah shoots at Harrison. "Amir, let me get on your shoulders!"

"That's not really what I had in mind," Rebecca says, rolling her eyes.

Amir claps Noah on the back. "Yeah, we can take 'em."

Dean splashes the group. "So, it's Rebecca and Harrison versus Amir and Noah. I'll ref again!" This time, he says the word *ref* a bit more softly—I'm guessing so that his voice doesn't break.

I give him a smile. Seems like he's going through some changes too, which kinda makes me feel better.

Noah jumps on Amir, and the next chicken-fight game begins.

During the momentary distraction, I turn to Lily and whisper quietly, "I think I might run to the bathroom. Just to double confirm that the tampon string hasn't slipped out of my bathing suit or anything."

"Oh. My. Gosh," a voice says from behind us. "Tahlia! Did you get your period?"

My stomach drops to my toes, and my knees wobble.

I know that voice.

Jackie has overheard my secret.

I'm doomed.

CHAPTER FOURTEEN

Lily and I slowly pivot to see Jackie swimming behind us, grinning.

"You started your period?" Jackie repeats. Thankfully, her voice is much quieter this time.

I shoot Lily a "please save me" look. Lily gives me an apologetic grimace.

This is horrible. Completely horrible. Jackie is going to ruin everything. This is more ammo for her to whip out whenever she wants to make fun of me, just like she did with the goggles and board shorts yesterday. Only this is much, *much-much* worse. This is my *period* we're talking about. It's like I've handed over top-secret information to the enemy.

Here you go, Jackie! Feel free to embarrass me with this whenever you'd like!

Jackie is still looking at me, waiting for an answer.

Do I lie? Laugh it off? Pretend to have suddenly broken my leg?

I decide lying is probably worse than telling her the truth. She'd scoff in my face, thinking I made the whole thing up. Then she'd tell people I only pretended to get my period, which, somehow, would be even worse.

"Um, yeah. I did," I answer softly.

Water splashes on my back from the chicken fight behind us, reminding me just how close we are to everyone else. They could easily overhear our conversation.

I want to sink under the water and away from Jackie's prying questions.

"Welcome to the Period Club!" Jackie pulls me into a hug. "When?"

I'm so stunned by the hug, I can't process what she's asked.

Suddenly, I'm convinced I'm still asleep next to Lily and this is all one big, strange dream, where Noah gives me a nickname and Jackie isn't rude.

Jackie is still grinning when she asks again, "Tahlia, when?"

I check over my shoulders to make sure everyone else is still paying attention to the chicken-fight game and not listening to us.

When I'm sure it's safe, I cautiously answer, "Yesterday. But, can we not talk about this right here?"

Jackie nods. "Totally! Let's go up to the pool deck." She wades over to the ladder, climbs out, and motions for Lily and me to follow.

If I'm not asleep, then Jackie must've hit her head on the bottom of the pool. She hasn't been this enthusiastic to talk with me in a year. It makes me wary to trust anything she says.

I reluctantly follow her, just wanting to get this conversation as far away from the group as possible.

Lily and I both climb out of the water and walk over to where Jackie has set down her stuff on a pool chair. She plops down in one of the chairs, and we take seats beside her. Luckily, the rest of them are still playing chicken fights and haven't yet realized that we've left the pool.

"Soooo, tell me all about it!" Jackie squeals.

Lily and I exchange another weirded-out look. Who is this person?

"Yeah, so, I started my period yesterday," I say, trying to figure out how I can give her as little information as possible. "And I figured out how to put in a tampon."

Jackie's eyes widen. "That's super impressive. It took me months to figure tampons out," she says. "Had to wear pads for so long." She waves. "But you guys know that. I must've told you last year."

Lily nods.

"Right..." I trail off, picking at my nails.

"You're so lucky that you used one on your first day." Jackie smiles. "I could tell you so many stories about when I was switching from pads to tampons. Seems like such a long time ago." She leans forward as if expecting me to respond.

I swallow and say, "Um, right, at first the tampon was really hard to use, but when I was relaxed, it was easier."

She playfully nudges my arm. "That's what happened to me too!"

"Really?"

"Yeah!"

I look between Lily and Jackie and realize how strangely comfortable I'm starting to feel. Our little group feels normal, which, in turn, feels odd. Have I been misreading Jackie's comments for the last few months? She's acting like we've never stopped being friends at all.

"And you're wearing the same tampon now?" Jackie asks. "What time did you put it in?"

"Yeah, I am," I say, feeling myself loosening up a bit. "I put it in around four in the morning. The box said I could leave it in for eight hours, so I should still be okay for a bit."

"Eight hours!" Jackie's eyes go wide. "That's

way too long! I try to change mine every hour so I don't get toxic shock syndrome."

"Toxic shock *what*?" Lily and I say at the same time.

"*Syndrome*," Jackie repeats. "Basically, if you have a tampon in too long, your vagina will shrivel up and then you die." She shrugs as if this is common knowledge.

"What?!" I reel back. "Are you serious?"

Jackie pushes her hair behind her ears. "Oh yeah. There's a warning about it on all the tampon boxes and everything. You didn't see it?"

I exchange a glance with Lily.

"No, I didn't see that," I admit.

"Me neither," Lily says, shaking her head.

"You should go change your tampon now. You know, just to be safe," Jackie says. "I'll wait here for you to get back."

"But"—I look from Jackie to Lily—"I don't *have* any more tampons with me. If I take out this one, I won't be able to get back in the pool."

Jackie reaches over to her bag. "I have one

you can use," she says. She pulls a long, yellow wrapped package from her bag and holds it out for me to take.

I shoot a look at the pool to make sure no one is watching us.

Jackie catches my uncertainty. "Oh, you don't want it?" she asks.

I stare at the tampon in her hand. "I'm just not sure I'll be able to, you know, figure out how to use it again."

Jackie furrows her brow. "Why not?"

My palms start to sweat. This isn't a conversation I want to be having at Noah's pool party. Or at all, really.

"It's just"—I look over my shoulder to triple-check no one can hear me—"I couldn't get the tampons to slide in. I think I only finally got one to work on a fluke."

Jackie cracks a smile, and I instantly feel like she's about to make fun of me. Why in the world is she smiling? She shouldn't be smiling at a time like this—I might have a *syndrome*!

But she doesn't make fun of me. Instead, she asks, "Did your tampons have a cardboard applicator?" Jackie crosses her arms.

I look to Lily.

We both look at Jackie.

"Uh, yes?"

"Well, there's your problem!" Jackie laughs and flips her hair.

I narrow my eyes at her. "How so?"

"Tahlia!" She chastises me with another nudge to my shoulder. "You can't *start* with a cardboard applicator! That's like, so hard. Even I still use tampons with plastic applicators." She laughs again. "I wish I could use the kind without an applicator altogether because, you know, those are better for the environment and all, but plastic is the best for beginners. At least that's what my mom says."

All I can do is stare at her. My brain is too busy unpacking everything that's happening. Jackie is giving me period tips.

Me.

The girl she ditched and has been rude to ever since.

It's confusing. Is she just being nice? Or is she trying to be friends with us again?

The thought fills me with an unexpected warmth.

But I don't even want to be friends with Jackie. Do I? Jackie rejected me. Well, *us*. Lily and me.

So then why do I suddenly feel kinda relieved that she's being nice again? My whole plan was to make Noah and others think I was fun to hang out with. Not *her*.

Although...

Maybe I have been missing my friendship with her. Everything started to change when she left our little group. Things were easier back then—back before Noah's party last year. It wasn't until the pool party that things started to get all strange and different.

Before the party, Jackie never seemed to care that Lily and I wore clothes like board shorts and goggles. She just liked us for being us. But then after the party, there seemed to be more rules. Rules that were not told to Lily and me.

I gulp. This is all too much to think about.

I have no idea why Jackie is acting like the last year didn't happen, but honestly, right now I don't mind. It's nice just to talk to her again like we used to.

This party is turning out better than I could have ever dreamed. I'm not some big joke everyone can laugh at, my period didn't stop me from getting in the water, and it seems like Lily and I might possibly have more friends next year.

I grin.

"Thanks, Jackie," I say.

" 'Course!"

I'm about to take the tampon from Jackie and walk to the bathroom, but before I do, I ask her the question that's nagging in the back of my mind. "Why are you being so nice to us? I—I thought you didn't want to be friends with us anymore."

Jackie frowns, and I instantly regret saying anything.

She chews the inside of her lip, thinking.

Lily looks at me with wide, stunned eyes.

"It's not that I didn't want to be friends with you guys anymore," Jackie starts to explain. "It's just, you guys...I don't know." She looks uncomfortable. "We just didn't really like the same things anymore"—she shrugs—"and you, well..."

"Weren't cool enough?" I offer with a half chuckle, saying her unspoken words.

She perks up, happy not to have been the one to say it. "Yeah!" She bites her lip. "Okay, that sounds mean, but you guys get it, right? We all know how we used to be, wearing those horrible one-piece suits like we were in elementary school and never talking to boys other than your brothers." She giggles.

"Oh, sure." I nod, unsure of what else to say. It's nice to finally have an explanation, but... it hurts, even if it's what I suspected. Last year I didn't even know we weren't cool. At least not until Noah's party. I thought we all still liked our suits and hanging out with just the three of us.

"But we're older now, yeah? I can tell," she says, smiling. "Eighth grade is going to be so fun." Jackie turns to Lily and pouts. "I wish you were going to be there, Lil." She runs a hand down Lily's arm.

Lily freezes and shoots a wary glance at me.

I suck in a deep breath, convinced I must've heard Jackie wrong. "What do you mean?"

Behind us, I can hear our classmates getting out of the pool. Their voices are getting closer and closer—they must be walking toward us. I wish they would stay in the pool and far away from this conversation.

Lily's face drops. It almost looks like she pities me.

"What does she mean?" I ask Lily directly.

Jackie looks confused. "Lily is moving to Maryland. You know, before her new baby sibling comes?"

She must notice my dumbfounded expression, because she adds, "Didn't you know?"

I can feel the color drain from my face as if the wind has just been knocked out of me.

I ignore Jackie and zero in on Lily. "You're moving to Maryland?" I make *Maryland* sound like a dirty word.

There's a gasp from behind me. Our other classmates must've heard me.

Jackie mumbles under her breath, "Oh, I guess she didn't know."

Lily looks down at her fingernails and begins to pick at them. "Um, yeah. I kinda am," she confesses. "My dad was offered a new job, and Mom thought that with the new baby coming, it was the right time to move." She doesn't look up at me.

My vision starts to blur, and I struggle to maintain a slow breath.

"When did this happen?" I ask a bit too loudly. "Why didn't you tell me?"

Our classmates start to gather in a circle around us. I can tell they're waiting to watch my soon-to-be meltdown.

Lily looks down at her hands again. "Well, it wasn't really official until a week or two ago. But yesterday was when my parents started packing up boxes. That's what I was doing when you called me yesterday—packing up. My parents wanted me to finish packing my room before the movers come next week."

"A week or so? A full week?!" I know that I'm

starting to sound a bit deranged, but I can't help it. I feel my cheeks going hot.

I want to stop talking and have this conversation away from all the nosy eyes looking on, but I can't stop the words from tumbling out of my mouth. "You've known for a week and didn't tell me?"

Everything this means begins to hit me like a tree branch to the face.

It means I won't see her all the time.

It means I'll no longer be able to walk to her house.

It means she won't be able to race over if I have another period emergency.

It means we won't have any more sleepovers.

And it means—

Oh. No.

I'll have to start eighth grade *alone*.

My head starts spinning, and all the faces staring at me begin to swirl together. I think I might faint right here with everyone watching.

It's at this very second that Noah walks into the circle, carrying boxes of pizza.

"I've got pizza! Who wants a slice without meat, and who wants—" Noah stops, clearly feeling the tension in the circle. "What's going on?" he asks.

"Tahlia just found out Lily's moving," Jackie announces.

Jackie's voice snaps me out of my dizzy trance. I blink until everyone's face returns to normal.

"Honestly, I thought she knew," Jackie adds.

Be quiet, Jackie! Every good thought I've ever had about Jackie goes up in flames in my mind. She is not my friend. She's made that pretty clear.

"Oh..." Noah grimaces.

Clearly, he knew too. It's obvious. They pity me. Everyone stares at me with sad, knowing eyes. They all knew about the move. Except me. I was the only one in the dark.

Tears start to well up in my eyes, and I have to wipe my nose to stop a sniffle. This is the exact feeling I was trying to avoid at this party—embarrassment. Never did I think that Lily would be the cause of it.

Lily stands up from the chair. "Come on, let's

go inside to talk." She tries to reach for my arm, but I pull back.

"No," I sniffle. "I'm fine. There's nothing to talk about," I lie.

I'm on the brink of a full-on meltdown. I need to get out of here before I make a huge scene in front of everyone.

"I—I just need to go to the bathroom," I manage to say without breaking into sobs.

I race into the house and hurry to the bathroom, forgetting all about grabbing the tampon from Jackie.

Thirty seconds later, there's a tap on the bathroom door.

"Tahlia?"

It's Lily. I don't respond.

She continues, "I was going to tell you. Honestly, I was. I tried to bring it up yesterday, I really did. This is not how you were supposed to find out. I just..." She doesn't finish her sentence.

I hate it when she does this. She'll start a sentence knowing full well I'm interested in what she has to say, but when she gets to the good bits, she always trails off, as if she's checking to make sure I'm really listening. It gets me every time, and she knows it.

"You just *what*, Lily?" I reluctantly huff through the door.

"I just, I don't know. I tried telling you, but I just couldn't, I guess. And then this morning you said you didn't want anything to ruin your day, so I didn't want to say anything."

"But you had no problem whatsoever telling Jackie. Some best friend *you* are," I snap.

Lily doesn't respond, which is fine with me. I don't want to listen to anything she has to say anyway.

I sit on the floor across from the toilet.

"I thought..." She sighs. "I thought you could be friends with her again once I left. I didn't want to leave you alone. And I could obviously tell this party was super important to you, so I figured, I don't know, maybe you were trying to make up for last year or something and make Jackie like us again. I know how much that hurt you. But I don't know why I told her. I'm sorry." She taps the door again. “Just come out, okay? We can still have fun at the party.”

At this, I push up from the floor and fling open the door to look her dead in the eye.

“No. Just leave me alone,” I snap. “I might as well get used to being by myself. It’ll be good practice for when you leave.” Tears stream down my face. “And if you knew how much it hurt when Jackie stopped hanging out with us, then you wouldn’t be doing the same thing to me again! You clearly don’t care about our friendship!”

Lily’s face drops in shock. I don’t blame her. I’m just as surprised at the things I’m spewing. But now that the words are out of my mouth, I can’t take them back. That will make me look weak.

“You honestly think I don’t care?” she says softly.

“Yeah, do you need me to spell it out for you?” I double down on my attack. “If you *actually* cared about being my friend, you would’ve made your parents stay. That’s what I would’ve done for you!” My hands shake. I know what I’m saying is ridiculous, but I can’t stop.

"What are you talking about?!" Lily stares at me with wide eyes. "I've spent the last twenty-four hours running around town looking for tampons for you! How is that not caring about our friendship?" Her voice gets even louder.

"That's different!" I shoot back. "And friends who actually care about other friends don't let them find out that they're moving at a party!"

"As if *I'm* the only one not always caring about our friendship," she retorts.

"What is *that* supposed to mean?"

Lily scoffs. "You really don't know?"

"Be my guest. Inform me," I challenge.

"If you hadn't been so obsessed with this party and whatever, then maybe you would've noticed something was going on with me! All we talk about are *your* problems! It's always about you, you, *you*!" Her face flushes red. "Did you ever stop to think about me? No! Of course not!" She throws her hands up. "Because you're so self-centered. And a *coward*."

It feels like I've been slapped. "Oh, really? *I'm* the coward?" I sputter. "Well, you're too scared to tell me lots of things! For example, I know you like my brothers! You're too chicken to admit it! And the biggest one—you were too much of a coward to tell me you were moving!"

"I tried to tell you!" Lily balls her hands into fists. "I've been trying to tell you about the move for weeks! But every time I bring it up, you cut me off and the conversation goes back to something about you! Always about you!" she says, seething. "Then last night, I was going to tell you before we watched the movie, but I just couldn't. With everything that happened at the restaurant and your period, I just thought it wasn't the right time to bring it up!"

"Oh, sure, blame my period. As if *that's* not a coward move."

"Well—well," Lily sputters. "You're so much of a coward, you can't even tell your dad you need tampons!" she blurts back.

I clench my teeth. "Because he's my *dad*!"

"Exactly!" she snorts. "He's your dad! Obviously, he knows what periods are! I'd tell my dad. You're just a big chicken."

“That’s not true,” I sniffle. My eyes begin to fill with tears again.

“It is!”

“Just leave already, Lily,” I snap. “I don’t want you here.”

“Fine, I will!” she retorts. “I’m going back to the party.”

I want to slam the door, but it’s not even my house, so I can’t bang it closed like I would at home. I close it as angrily yet as softly as I can.

CHAPTER FIFTEEN

For the next fifteen minutes, I sit on the bathroom floor and silently cry.

I'm being ditched again. But this time it's by my best friend.

I lost Jackie, and now I've lost Lily. I have no friends. This party completely sucks.

The thought makes me cry even harder.

I replay the events from yesterday in my head, and they all start clicking into place. It makes sense why Lily didn't respond when I talked about starting eighth grade. And why she was acting weird to Jackie outside the grocery store. And why she was strange on the phone with her mom. And why she cried during the movie. It *all* makes sense.

She was keeping this massive secret from me.

I use the back of my hands to wipe my dripping nose.

And on top of all that, everything I've planned for the party is ruined. It is a total disaster and so much worse than last year. I would take being called "Baby Goggles" for another year over being known as the friendless girl who was crying in the bathroom. So much for new and improved! More like pathetic and weird.

I drop my head into my hands, and my shoulders bob up and down with my sobs.

After a while, someone comes by and jiggles the doorknob, trying to use the bathroom, but before I get up off the floor to open it to tell them to go away, I hear someone mumble to them, "Tahlia is in there!" Which makes the jiggling stop and makes me feel even worse.

The longer I sit on the floor, the harder it is to get up to leave. At this point, I'm too embarrassed to show my face in the hallway *and* too embarrassed to stay locked in a bathroom at Noah's house. There are no good options. Maybe I can tunnel my way home.

I know I need to get out. I don't even know if Noah's house has a second bathroom for the other party guests to use. People with small bladders may be close to exploding, for all I know. Every second I stay in here just makes everything more terrible.

Before I muster the courage to leave the bathroom, I stand up from the floor and take a last look into the mirror.

I still have curly hair sticking out in every direction, I still have pink-and-blue braces, and I still have a terrible, ugly sunburn peeling on my nose. Basically, nothing has changed from yesterday.

Except now my best friend is moving. *And* she thinks I'm a self-centered coward. *And* I'm going to be made fun of at school. *And* I'm friendless.

Another lump rises in my throat, and I have to hold my breath to keep from crying again. I just need to make it home. If I can get out of this bathroom and home, I can cry as loudly as I want in my own bedroom.

When I finally twist the knob on the bathroom door, I half expect to see Lily just outside the door, waiting for me to emerge. I hitch in a little breath of anticipation of facing her.

But when I step out, she's not there. And I don't blame her. The terrible things I said to her make my mouth sting when I think of them. I'm not even sure if I'm disappointed or relieved she's not there.

I go with relieved. I'm not ready to see her again just yet.

There's laughter coming from the kitchen. They must've brought the pizza inside to eat.

I head to the left and hope that by some miracle, I can sneak back out to the pool and grab my bag without being seen. Yet as soon as I take a step to the left, I smack my forehead directly into someone with a loud thunk.

We both make an *oomph!* noise, and towels tumble to the ground from the arms of the person I've just bumped into. As I rub my forehead, I look through my fingers to see that it's Noah, which makes me want to crawl under the carpet.

"Oh, hey, Tahls," he says cautiously. I can tell he's wary of me. He's probably waiting for me to start crying.

I wish he would drop the stupid nickname. I don't deserve it.

"I'm sorry," I say as we both bend down to pick up the towels. "I got turned around and went left instead of right. I thought..." I trail off. I don't want to admit to him I've just been crying in his bathroom—even though I'm sure he already knows. He saw my dramatic exit.

"I was just grabbing a few towels," he says awkwardly. "Amir and Dean forgot theirs, even though I reminded them to bring one." He rolls his eyes.

I give my best "everything is fine" smile and ask, "Is your head okay?"

Noah rubs his forehead. "Yeah, it's okay. Are *you* okay?"

I rub my forehead too. "Yeah, I'm fine," I say, even though I most certainly am NOT fine. Another image of me sitting by myself at lunch flashes into my mind. I suck in a breath.

Must. Not. Cry.

"Good," he says, chuckling uncomfortably. Of course, he is fully aware that someone who was just holed up in his bathroom for the last twenty minutes is far from okay, but I appreciate him for not asking about it further. I don't want to talk about it. If he can pretend, I can pretend. We can both pretend we're at a normal pool party with no tears, no periods, no moving best friends, and no *self-centered cowards* like me. We're all just having a perfectly fun time, and everything isn't changing without our permission.

I sigh, and he raises an eyebrow. He probably thinks I'm about to start tearing up again. I feel like I might.

He probably doesn't think I'm that cool anymore. Not after all my crying.

Maybe I should try to get him to like me one more time, just to see if it changes anything. I don't have anything more to lose at this point.

"Hey, Noah?" I say, sucking in my impending

tears. My heart thumps in my chest. I feel like I'm about to take a plunge off a gigantic cliff.

"Yeah?" He raises an eyebrow.

My voice quavers as I ask my perfect saved line. "Isn't it random our parents work together?" It doesn't come out as relaxed and fun as I've imagined. It's forced and sad. "How random is that?" I add and attempt a laugh, but that also comes out flat. I'm not really in a laughing mood.

Noah smiles, but it doesn't reach his eyes. "So weird," he agrees and tosses the towels over his shoulder.

I stare at him, waiting for him to say more.

But that's it. That's all he says.

I feel like I've been punched in the gut as all my perfect Noah conversations come tumbling down around me. I've wasted my perfect line.

This day can't get any worse.

Noah rubs the back of his neck. "Well, we're all eating in the kitchen. My mom brought out some ice cream. I think we're going to get back in the pool soon, though. Coming?" He motions down the hall toward where the laughter is coming from.

I give him a forced half smile. There is no way I am going in there and facing Lily. "Oh, um, yeah. I'll be right behind you," I quietly lie. I don't want to tell him that I'm about to leave his party.

"Okay! See you there," he says as he turns and walks back toward the party.

And I'm left standing in the hallway feeling completely, utterly, 100 percent alone.

I can no longer be anywhere near this party. I'm the girl who didn't know her best friend was moving. How pathetic is that? I bet they're all in there giggling about it now.

With the image of them all laughing in my head, I hurry through the living room, hoping no one spots me hustling past the kitchen, and go back outside to grab my stuff. Then I do something I never thought I'd do. I pull out my phone from my bag, take a deep breath, and call Dad.

It takes three rings for him to pick up.

"Tahlia? Everything okay?" Dad says before even saying hello. Stupid caller ID. He's not used to me calling and most likely isn't expecting any type of communication from me during Noah's party.

"Can you come pick me up?" I hiccup into the phone.

"Of course. Why?" Then he adds, "Are kids doing things they aren't supposed to be doing?"

"*No*, Dad," I whine.

There's a pause before he responds. I picture him on the other end of the phone, narrowing his eyes and scratching his chin. I'm sure he's probably just trying to determine how serious this situation is.

"I'll be there soon," he finally answers.

"Thanks," I hiccup again.

I stuff the phone back into my bag and sneak my way out Noah's front door. I don't say goodbye to anyone.

Ten minutes later, I'm sitting on the curb in front of Noah's house when Dad's car rolls around the corner. When he pulls the car to the curb, I stand up and brush off my butt before yanking open the back door and climbing inside.

"Should I wait for Lily?" Dad asks as I buckle myself in.

"No."

He frowns. "Okay. Is the party wrapping up?" he asks. I know *he* knows what time the party is meant to end, so I suspect he just wants to get more information out of me.

"Nope."

He narrows his eyes at me in the rearview mirror. "So you just wanted to come home?"

"Yup."

"Ah, one-syllable answers only. Got it."

I don't respond. Technically, silence isn't one syllable.

"Want to sit up here in the front?" He points to the passenger seat.

Oh, he's good. *Real* good. That's the one question he knows will get a reaction out of me. I ask to sit up front all the time, and my parents always say no. He's using his smug parenting skills on me, and I can't even fight it, because even when my brothers aren't in the car, my parents still insist I sit in the back because it's "safer" and makes them "feel at ease." It's a load of baloney.

I know exactly what he's doing by asking that question—he's trying to get me to *engage*—yet I have no power to stop my excitement. I am too weak to resist the front seat.

"Really?" I ask with a raised brow, playing right into his trap.

"Yeah, why not?" He pats the seat. "Just don't tell Mom."

"I won't," I say as I scramble over the middle seats and buckle into the front.

"Buckled?" he asks.

"Buckled," I confirm.

"Good."

He pulls the car away from the curb, and I watch Noah's house get smaller and smaller in the passenger mirror. I wonder if they've started playing Truth or Dare. I bet Lily is telling them all even more secrets I don't know.

I let out a sad huff.

"So, you want to tell me why you're being

picked up early?" Dad asks, then adds, "You don't have to, you know. Only if you want."

I sigh and look out the window. "I don't want to."

"Okay."

We continue down the road in silence. I let my forehead rest against the glass. Every time we hit a bump in the road, my head bounces on the window. It hurts, but I don't move it. I like the cold glass against my face.

Self-centered and *coward* flash over and over again in my head. I close my eyes, but it doesn't stop me from hearing Lily's words. I wrap my arms around my midsection to stop the hurt.

The words probably wouldn't hurt so much if they weren't true, my stupid inner voice smugly jabs at me. I don't have a good retort for it. The voice is right—Lily's words *are* true. She was trying to tell me something, but I was just too... what? Too wrapped up in my own problems to care? Too focused on being cool at a dumb pool party? Too needy of Lily to drop everything and focus on me?

Yes, the voice answers. *All of the above.*

I tell the voice to kindly shut the heck up. It doesn't. It continues to repeat Lily's words in my head. *Self-centered. Coward.*

With annoyance I remember I stupidly didn't even grab the tampon Jackie offered me, so I'm basically in the exact same situation I started in yesterday. Well, worse, really, because yesterday at this time I still had Lily and some hope that the party would be better than last year's.

Once Dad and I get home, I guess I could use one of the pads from Mom hidden in my desk and then sneak into her bathroom to grab more, but deep down I know I'm not going to. There's only so long I can create plans and keep my period a secret from Dad before it gets too tiring. And I'm tired. Really, really tired.

I don't want to sneak anymore. I just want to flop on my bed and cry until Mom comes home.

However, even though I am tired, I'm still going to need more products soon. My period doesn't care that Mom is out of town.

It suddenly dawns on me that I already know exactly what I'm going to do. I think I've known since I got in the car. I don't want to be self-centered. I don't want to be a coward. I close my eyes and take a deep breath. My blood pounds in my ears, and my hands start to feel sweaty.

"Dad?" I say, still keeping my forehead balancing on the window.

"Yeah?"

I don't answer right away. My mouth has to catch up with my brain. Once I do this, there is no turning back.

The car engine hums as we turn onto the next street.

My forehead is starting to ache from the bumps against the window, so I lean back in the seat and fiddle with a loose string on my jean shorts.

Dad's still waiting for me to say something. I can't let the silence stretch on any longer. The quiet is worse than just saying what I need to say.

Don't be a coward, I repeat over and over in my head.

Before I have the chance to second-guess and stop myself, I blurt, "Dad, I started my period, and

I need to buy products. Can we stop at the store on our way home?"

My words hang in the air. My heart thumps in my chest. I think I might start crying again.

Dad shifts his weight in the seat. He keeps his right hand on the wheel while using his left to rub the back of his neck.

I clench my jaw and brace for one of his stupid jokes. A knot in my stomach makes me lean forward in my seat. If he laughs or makes any type of joke, I think I'll be sick.

But instead, he clears his throat and says, "We don't need to stop."

It's such an odd response, I'm not sure how to react. Maybe he didn't hear what I just said.

"But I—" I start.

He holds up a hand. "Let me finish." He clears his throat again. "We don't need to stop *because* I already went out and bought you everything you need. It's under the sink in your bathroom."

I stare at him with wide, confused eyes as his statement sinks in. The knot in my stomach slowly begins to untwist.

"What? When? How did you—?" The questions tumble out of my mouth.

"I went while you were at the party," he says, smiling.

"But how did you know?" I ask, horrified. I rack my brain for any possible explanation. I'm not sure if I should be embarrassed or not. Did I leave something bloody out for him to see? Did he catch me in a lie? Or, worse—did Mary Ann from the grocery store call him and tell him what happened?

Dad chuckles. "Because dads know everything."

I narrow my eyes at him. "Dad," I warn. I am *not* in the mood to be messed with.

He sighs. "And because I went into your bathroom to take out the trash and saw about ten unwrapped tampons buried in the bottom of it."

"Oh..." I stare down at my hands. "Right."

There's another beat of silence.

"I'm sorry you felt like you couldn't tell me," Dad says softly.

I wiggle uncomfortably. I don't have a lot of talks like this with Dad. It's strange.

"No, it's not that." I pick at one of my nails and lower my voice. "It's just embarrassing, okay?"

He doesn't answer right away. We both stare out the windshield to watch a family cross the road in front of our car.

It's quiet in the car as he adjusts his grip on the wheel.

"Nothing about your body is embarrassing, Tahlia," he says, still staring straight ahead.

I look down at my hands. A little hiccup escapes from my chest.

This is not a conversation I woke up today thinking I'd be having. It's a little odd and a bit too personal, but strangely, it's kinda exactly what I need.

"Okay." I nod. I hiccup again.

"Unless you get a funny sunburn." Dad smiles. "Then you *should* be embarrassed about your sunscreen application, and I *will* laugh." He chuckles. "Fair warning."

I grin as I realize it's the first time I've felt truly relaxed since I got my period. It feels like a massive rock has been lifted off my chest and I'm breathing normally again. I no longer have to lie or sneak around. I can just be, well, me. And I will not be a coward anymore.

But then the rock settles back down on my chest when I think about Lily.

I sigh and fold my arms across my stomach. I think I might throw up.

"Is there something else?" Dad asks.

I might as well tell him. It's not like I have friends to talk with anymore.

"Lily's moving," I say softly.

He hums in understanding. "And you just found out?"

I nod but don't say anything.

"I see."

He's not acting surprised, like I thought he would. I'm dropping huge news and he's acting like it's no big deal.

"Wait!" I sit up and turn to face him. "Did *you* know?"

"Her parents might have shared the news with me, yes."

"And you didn't tell me either!" I groan.

He doesn't answer.

I rest my head on the back of the seat. "She's leaving me just like Jackie did." The pathetic words tumble out before I'm able to stop them.

Dad sighs. "Tahlia, it's nothing like that. Lily's dad was offered an incredible job. It's not a reflection on you. Not at all. This is what's best for her family."

I chew my bottom lip. When he says it like that, it makes me feel even worse for the things I said to Lily.

"Okay?" he says.

"Okay," I sadly agree, knowing he's right.

With a huff, I settle into the passenger seat, and we drive the rest of the journey in comfortable silence.

CHAPTER SIXTEEN

Dad gently shakes my shoulder and I blink open my eyes. Somehow, I've managed to fall asleep during the last few minutes of the drive home. My cheek is sore from resting against the car door.

Sigh. I'll probably never get to sit in this seat again until I'm thirty. It was good while it lasted.

I climb out of the car and follow Dad through the garage into the house before marching upstairs to my bedroom. Even though I've solved the problem of getting products without Mom, I still have the huge problem of Lily moving away hanging over my head. Not to mention all the horrible things I said to her. We've fought before, but never like *that*.

Before I close the door to my bedroom, I decide to sneak a quick peek across the hall at the cabinet under the sink in the bathroom where Dad said he put all the products. Needing to see them with my own eyes, I hustle over and swing the cabinet door open. Sure enough, boxes upon boxes of various period products are stacked in neat little rows. Dad even bought the plastic-applicator tampons Jackie had.

I sigh in relief.

I want to tell Lily about the boxes of tampons. I want to tell her all about my conversation with Dad and how brave I was to let him know about my period. She wouldn't think I was a coward if she knew.

I wish I could say to Lily, *Holy Mother of Uncle Harold! Look at all these grown-up products under the sink!* And Lily would say, *You got that right, Tahlia. So many boxes!*

But I can't. Lily probably doesn't want to talk to me after everything I said to her.

And that really, really stinks.

I'm about to flop onto my bed and cry when my phone vibrates in my pocket. A little spark of hope makes me think it could be Lily calling, but when I look at the caller ID, Mom's picture flashes on the screen. I click the green Accept button as fast as I can.

"Mom!" I half shout, half choke into the phone.

"Hi, honey," she says. I can tell by her tone that my greeting surprised her. "I just drove back into service. How are you? Are you still at the party?"

"I-started-my-period-and-Lily-is-moving-and-Noah's-party-was-terrible-and-I-ruined-my-jeans-with-a-virgin-margarita!" I garble the sentence so quickly into the phone, it comes out sounding like one long word. I don't even try to stop the tears that begin to drip down my face.

There is a beat before she says, "Wait, what? Say that one more time. I couldn't understand any of that."

"I started my period, and Lily's moving!" I sob into the phone.

"Oh, Tahlia," Mom coos.

"*And* I'm infected with toxic shock syndrome!" I continue to cry, remembering I've left my tampon in for more than eight hours.

The tears make it hard for me to take a breath. I take a big gulp of air.

"Wait, what?" Mom asks. "Honey, you do not have toxic shock syndrome."

"But I do!" I wail. "Jackie told me I had to change my tampon every hour, or I'd get toxic shock whatever, and I left in a tampon for too long and—" I suck in another gulp of air. My chest is starting to feel tight.

"Take a deep breath," Mom soothes. "In through your nose, out through your mouth."

I do as she says, but the tears won't stop.

"Tahlia, listen to me." Her voice is firm but reassuring. "You do not need to change a tampon every hour, okay? Toxic shock syndrome can happen, but it's rare. I'd only be seriously concerned if you left your tampon in for more than a day and you started to run a fever."

"Yeah, but—"

"Yeah, but *nothing*. You just need to learn your flow. You'll get used to it, sweetheart. We can go over all the period stuff when I get home tonight. Don't you worry."

I snivel and wipe my eyes with the heels of my hands.

"Now," she continues, "about Lily moving—"

"I'm not going to have any friends!" I blurt. "I'm going to be all alone! How could she do this to me—just like Jackie!"

I hear Mom take a deep breath. "Just because Lily is moving doesn't mean you won't remain friends." Her voice is calm and measured. "And we can sign you up for more extracurriculars next year so you can make even more friends."

"But Lily is moving to *Maryland*," I say with another sob. "And I don't want different friends."

"Grandma Judy lives in Maryland, and you see her every month."

"Yes, but it won't be the *same*!"

"I know, Tahlia. I know," she sighs. "These are big changes, and it's sad, but things aren't supposed to remain the same. Getting your period, expanding your friend circle—that's all part of life."

"Well, this part of life sucks," I grump.

"I realize it feels like that right now, but I have no doubt that you will remain friends with Lily. You guys love each other. Different states won't change that."

I sniffle.

"Do you know when she's moving?" Mom asks. "Maybe you could have her over for a sleepover or something before she goes. That would be fun."

"Next week," I groan. It might as well be tomorrow. One week is barely any time at all. I had so many more summer plans for us.

I gulp and my hands go all tingly. How am I going to survive without Lily? I'll be completely lost without her and—

No! that tiny voice inside my head injects. Of course Lily cares about our friendship. And all I was doing was worrying about myself. Lily was right. I should've paid more attention to her. She clearly was trying to tell me something, and I was only focused on getting the cool kids to like me.

I wipe my nose with the back of my hand.

"Ah, next week. So soon," Mom says. "Well, then you should definitely invite her over. I'm sure she's not looking forward to making new friends in a new state."

A lightbulb flashes in my mind.

Lily isn't going to have her best friend with her either. I can't make this all about me. Lily is the one moving after all. She needs me.

I need to talk to Lily. Now.

A plan begins to form in my head—I need to apologize to Lily as soon as possible, and I don't have time to waste. I can't let her move away like this. I'll have to just run over to her house and wait for her to get home from the party.

Mom is right. I'll always be friends with Lily—that is, if she ever forgives me for what I said at the party.

Thinking of the party, I add, "By the way, you should've told me to start with tampons that had plastic applicators!" I huff into the phone to Mom. "Those cardboard and bullet ones are the worst!"

"Bullet tampons?" Mom questions. "What in the world are bullet tampons?"

"I don't have time to explain. Talk tonight."

"Wait, Tahlia—"

I end the call before she finishes. The quicker I get to Lily's house, the quicker I can make this right. Our last few precious days of living close to each other can't feel like this.

Before I go, I grab one of the tampon boxes from under the sink, then hustle down the stairs.

"Dad!" I call.

He pops his head out from the kitchen. "What?"

"I'll be right back. I'm going over to Lily's."

He eyes the box in my hand but doesn't question any further. "Okay. Call if you plan to stay late." He smiles.

"I will!" I shout over my shoulder, already making my way out the front door.

Even though Lily is probably still at Noah's party, that doesn't stop me from running the entire way to her house. I'll wait all night on her front steps for her to get home if I need to.

When I finally run up Lily's driveway, I plop

myself down on her porch and keep my eyes on the road to look out for her family car bringing her home.

A creaking sound startles me from behind, and I turn to see Lily's mom poking her head out the door. When she looks down and sees me, she says, "Oh, hi, honey! I thought I saw you race by the window."

As Mrs. Baek opens the door wider, my eyes settle on her pregnant belly. The baby must've doubled in size since the last time I saw Lily's mom.

I scramble to my feet. "Hi, Mrs. Baek. Is Lily back from the party?"

"Oh yes! She's in her room," Lily's mom says. "She wasn't feeling well and had to leave the party early, poor thing. I was in the middle of packing up all this stuff and had to stop what I was doing to pick her up. We actually just got back." She pauses. "Wait, weren't you supposed to be at the party too? Did you also leave early?"

I shove my hands into my pockets. "Oh, uh, yeah, I was, but... I wasn't feeling too well either," I say.

Mrs. Baek crosses her arms across her chest as best she can—her pregnant belly makes it a little hard. "Maybe they were serving some food that had gone bad."

"I don't think that was it," I say quickly, not wanting the Campos family to be accused of giving us spoiled snacks.

"Well, anyways, come in!" Lily's mom motions for me to step inside.

I follow her through the front door, and it immediately becomes clear why Lily didn't want me seeing the inside of her house this morning.

All the furniture has been replaced with large boxes stacked on even larger boxes. Pictures have been taken off the walls, leaving faint outlines where they used to hang, and the rugs are rolled up and leaning in a corner. The floor is mostly bare, aside from a few flat boxes and packing-tape dispensers.

Lily's mom puts a hand on my shoulder. "When she's feeling better, can you tell Lily I need her to come out and tell me which of these old toys she wants me to keep?" She holds up a couple of dolls with choppy haircuts.

"Sure, Mrs. Baek," I say before slowly walking toward Lily's room.

I take a deep breath with every step.

When I'm finally outside her room, Lily's door is ajar, so I warily push it open. Lily sits cross-legged on her bed, surrounded by piles of random objects—some old books, some photographs, and some old dress-up clothes. Like the living room, Lily's room is piled high with boxes.

"Hi," I say and give her a timid half smile.

Lily looks up from the piles. "Hi," she says back. Her eyes look like she's been crying too.

"Looks like we both left the party early." I force out a chuckle and rub the back of my neck. "How is packing going?"

Lily tosses one of her old toys into a box labeled **DONATE**.

"It's okay." She shrugs.

"Need any help?"

Lily stops what she's doing to raise an eyebrow

at me. "Why would *you* want to help *me*?" she shoots. "Thought I didn't 'care about our friendship' enough for you."

"Well, I..." I pause, wanting my next words to be perfect. I can't screw up this apology, since I only get one shot at it. There's not enough time for me to be a coward. If I don't apologize now, I know I'll regret it.

I muster all my courage. "I'm really sorry about what I said, Lily. I don't know why I said all that." I rub the side of my arm. "I think I was just hurt and sad, so I was being mean. It's not a good excuse, but I know you care about our friendship. Of course I know that. You've always cared."

Lily nods her head and looks down at her hands. "But you still shouldn't have said what you did."

"I know," I sigh. "Again, I don't know why I even said all that."

"I do." Lily smirks. "It's because you're going to miss me, so you wanted to lash out and hurt me."

"Have you been reading your Mom's therapy books again?" I giggle.

"Maybe," she says, grinning.

We both chuckle.

Lily tucks her hair behind her ears. "I really am sorry you had to find out that way. I never wanted to do what Jackie did."

"I know," I say, nodding.

"And I'm sorry I called you self-centered and a coward, Tahlia," she says.

"That's okay. I kinda was."

Lily continues. "I guess I just didn't want to tell you I was moving because I didn't want it to be real—because if you didn't know, the more I could pretend. And once I told you, there'd be no turning back—it would really be happening—you understand?"

I sit on the edge of her bed. "I wish it wasn't real too."

"Then the longer and longer I waited to say anything, the harder it got to bring it up at all," she admits.

"I get it," I say.

"I'm sorry."

"Me too." I smile.

Lily pulls me in for a hug.

"Any chance we can convince your parents not to move?"

"I wish," she moans. "Already tried. My parents are more stubborn than I am."

"Then I'll text you every day," I declare. "And call, and send smoke signals, and mail letters by bird!"

Lily giggles. "You better. And when the baby comes, you better come down to meet them."

"Obviously!"

"And maybe we can watch *Jurassic Park* in my new living room when you come visit." Her smile fades into a frown. "But that'll only happen if my parents are too busy with the baby and don't notice what we're watching. They still don't like me watching PG-13."

"No!" I groan. "I'm not watching that movie again."

"I'm kidding, I'm kidding," she says, rolling her eyes.

"By the way," I say, remembering the tampon

box in my hand. "I brought you something. A going-away gift of sorts." I hand her the box.

She takes it and stares at me with awe. "Where did you get these?"

"My dad," I say. "I told him about my period, but it turns out he kinda already knew. And you were right, by the way, about me being a coward."

She giggles. "Yeah, you were. You even waded in a fountain so you didn't have to tell him. You literally waded in a fountain!"

"*You* told me to go in that fountain!" I scoff.

"Mainly so I could laugh at you." She smirks, but I know she's kidding. "But thank you for the tampons. I'll make sure to pack them with special care for whenever I actually need them."

"You better," I say, playfully nudging her shoulder. "And you better call me when it happens."

"Obviously I will." Lily nudges my shoulder.

We smile at each other.

Lily narrows her eyes at me. "Wait, Tahlia, what's that on your forehead?"

I bring my hand up to my head and feel a large bump.

Oh. My. God.

I spin around to look in the mirror behind Lily's door. There, smack-dab in the middle of my forehead, is another zit growing.

You've got to be kidding me.

Lily stands up from the bed with a smirk. "Come on," she says. "Let's go sort your pimple out."

I poke the red dot. "I'm pretty sure this sucker will take the rest of the day to get rid of. Think you can sleep over to help?"

She crosses her arms. "Yeah, I think I can talk my mom into that."

"Good," I say, smiling.

"Good," she agrees.

And we march out of her room, ready to take on whatever comes next.

EPILOGUE

"Wait, wait!" Mom frantically waves her arms as my brothers and I head toward the garage. "Squish together—I want to take a photo." She pulls her phone out of her pocket and holds it up at us.

I groan. Mom makes us do this every year. Usually, I don't mind, but today I'm too anxious to happily smile for a picture. It's the first time since kindergarten I won't be arriving at school with Lily, and I'm not looking forward to starting eighth grade without her.

Who am I going to sit with at lunch? Or walk with in the halls? Or partner up with in class?

Just thinking about it makes my hands sweat.

Sure, I've had most of the summer to get used to my best friend living in a different state, but today is different. Today I can't video chat with Lily for half the day and then distract myself from my lack of friends by going to annoy my brothers. I think Mom and Dad even started to feel sorry for me. Three weeks after Lily moved, my parents packed us all into the car and we took a road trip down to Maryland to visit Grandma Judy and to see Lily's new house and baby brother. It was great—until we had to leave.

I spent the rest of my summer lounging around and debating if I should reach out to Noah. It had seemed like he liked hanging out with me at his party. Although I wasn't exactly sure what I'd say to him even if I did reach out.

Hey! Sorry for ditching your party without saying goodbye! Hope you're having a good break!

Lily said I was being a coward, again, but I informed her there was a difference between being a coward and *strategically* waiting for the perfect text to pop into my head.

It just never did. Besides, if he wanted to hang out, he could've always reached out to *me.*

Sigh.

Today will also be the first time I see Jackie and all my other classmates who were at the pool party. The last time they saw me, I'd gone off to cry in a bathroom.

And it's the first year I've had to pack tampons, pads, and a special pair of leak-proof, period-absorbing underwear in my backpack. Mom told me that periods take a few years to regulate, so I may not always know when the red gift is going to arrive. Isn't that just *great*?

So, yeah, I've got much more important things to worry about than posing for a cheesy photo.

"Come on, Tahlia. Get in between your brothers," Mom says, motioning for us to move closer together.

I make a face and shimmy between the twins. They put their arms around my shoulders, and we reluctantly grin toward the phone.

"Nice," Dad says with a nod as he looks at the photo over Mom's shoulder. "You three just keep growing and growing," he sighs.

There he goes, getting all sentimental again. If we don't get out of here soon, he'll start bringing out the baby photos.

"Okay, we're leaving," Ryan says.

"Drive slow and safe," Mom instructs.

"And don't have the music too loud," Dad adds.

"We know," the twins moan.

Really, I should be the one moaning. *I'm* the one who has to be driven to school by my brothers, and I do not think they are ready for that type of responsibility. It's like my parents don't even care that they only just got their licenses. I'm the precious cargo, here!

Although being driven by my brothers is a bit better than riding my bike alone, I'll never admit that.

I follow my brothers into the garage and slide into the back seat of Mom's old Toyota. The twins agreed to take turns driving, and today, Jamie has the keys. He starts the car and backs it out into the street before taking off toward my school.

My stomach churns as I envision walking to my first eighth-grade class all by myself. Hopefully, Lily isn't feeling this nervous as she gets closer to her new school.

I pull my phone out of my backpack and swipe it open to write her a text.

I hope you have a good first day <3
Video chat after school?

I hit Send and lean back against the headrest. It's not long before the phone vibrates in my hand. I look down at Lily's text.

You too. 😊 And yes, definitely!
Call me as soon as you get home.

I smile. At least if my first day of eighth grade goes horribly, I'll still get to talk with Lily after school. That's one thing to look forward to.

A few minutes later, Jamie pulls the car to a stop in front of my middle school, and I unbuckle my seat belt.

"Hey, Tahlia, wait," Jamie says over his shoulder as I start to open the car door.

I raise an eyebrow and pause. "What?"

He shares a look with Ryan.

"What?" I repeat, now annoyed.

"Are you, uh, going to be okay today?" Jamie asks.

"Yeah, I'll be fine," I say in a knee-jerk reaction.

"No, really," says Ryan. "If you get lonely or whatever, you can always text us at lunch if you want someone to talk to." He shrugs.

I raise my eyebrows in surprise. "Oh, um, thanks," I say a bit awkwardly.

"All right, now get out. You're going to make us late, *Professor*," Jamie says, back to his bossy older-brother tone.

I roll my eyes and hustle out of the car. Then I pull my backpack higher on my shoulders. My middle school looms large ahead of me.

It looks the same, but it feels different. So much has changed since the last time I was here.

"Bye, Mom!" I hear Jackie call from the drop-off loop behind me.

I turn and watch as Jackie hops out of her car and heads toward the school. She doesn't stop to talk to me, which is fine. I don't have anything to say to her either. It's obvious we don't really have much in common these days.

Then I spot Rebecca Jordan, who seems to have gotten new pink earrings for eighth grade, talking to Harrison Lopez, who looks twice as tall as he did at the start of summer. They wave to some of our other classmates who are climbing out of their cars.

That's when I see Noah. He's gotten a tan and a haircut since I last saw him at his pool party, making him look even cooler. He walks over to where Rebecca and Harrison are standing.

Noah looks up and notices me. I suck in a breath.

"Hey, Tahls!" he calls as he waves me over to join their group.

I'm still Tahls! And he wants me to join them! I guess he doesn't care that I made a scene at his party. I could squeal!

I walk—no, *run*—over to them.

"Hi, Tahlia!" they say.

"Hi! How was your summer?" I ask, a bit too enthusiastically.

"Good!"

Noah turns to me and says, "Tahls, I *wish* I could've texted you while I was at sleepaway camp. You would've laughed so hard. There was a kid who..."

I can't even pay attention to the rest of what he says. I'm too focused on the fact that Noah wanted to text *me*. I try to keep from blushing.

"Oh, you went to camp?" I say, trying to sound nonchalant.

He nods. "Yeah. It was cool, except I had no phone service for, like, a month. What did you do over summer?"

My stomach does a loop-the-loop, and I'm about to share the only interesting thing about my summer—going to Maryland—when I see a girl I don't recognize standing alone near the water fountain. She doesn't look like a younger classman—she's super tall and has real, actual hips. Maybe she's new.

The girl timidly glances around as she tugs at the sleeves of her gray hoodie, which has a dinosaur wearing sunglasses on it. It makes me think of *Jurassic Park*, which makes me think of Lily.

Lily is going to flip when I tell her about these latest Noah developments. Or really, the *only* Noah developments.

I wonder if Lily is standing all alone at her new school right now. Hopefully not. If Lily is standing alone right now, it would be great if someone went up and talked to her. And I hope—

Oh man.

I look back at Noah. He's still waiting for me to answer his question. And I want to, I really do, but there's now something nagging at me.

I'm that someone, aren't I? If Lily were here, *she'd* go up to the new girl.

I tell Noah, "One sec," before heading toward the water fountain. I've waited a whole summer for a perfect conversation with Noah. I can wait a few minutes more.

The girl looks at me with wide eyes as I approach her.

"Hi, I'm Tahlia. Are you a new eighth grader here?" I ask with a smile.

The girl tucks her hair behind her ear and nods. "Yeah, my dad and I just moved here from Oregon. I'm Steph."

"Cool! I've never been to Oregon before."

"It's pretty great," she says, sounding a little sad.

"Want to meet some of our classmates?" I ask. I glance over my shoulder at Noah. He smiles as Rebecca and Harrison beckon us over. "Some of my friends," I amend.

Steph's face brightens as she nods again.

I introduce her to Rebecca, Harrison, and Noah. Soon Amir Abdi and Hannah Bean join our little group too. We continue to talk about our summers until the first bell rings.

Steph suddenly looks uncomfortable again, so I say, "Come on. Let's walk to class."

So we do. Together.

Acknowledgments

Almost like it went through puberty, this book grew and developed after many changes. I am eternally grateful for everyone who helped shape it into what it is today.

Jessica Mileo, agent extraordinaire, I am very lucky to be on this journey with you. Your guidance and support for both this book and my career are unmatchable. Thank you for taking a chance on an underwritten manuscript and for giving me the tools to develop as a writer.

My brilliant editor, Liz Kossnar. I feel like you were cosmically destined to work on this book. You just GET it. Thank you for effortlessly weaving the heart into the humor and for bringing *Tahlia* into the world.

Thank you to everyone at Little, Brown Books for Young Readers who helped champion this story, including Megan Tingley, Jackie Engel, Alvina Ling, Aria Balraj, Hannah Milton, Jenny Kimura, Jen Graham, Virginia Lawther, Emilie Polster, Shanese Mullins, Mara Brashem, Christie Michel, Cheryl Lew, Shawn Foster, Danielle Cantarella, Karen Torres, Claire Gamble, and many more. Thank you also to copyeditor Maureen Klier and cover artist Marta Kissi.

Melissa Seymour, you sweet ray of human sunshine, you. Thank you for being my partner in publishing. Genuinely unsure how I'd survive the writing life without you.

Alyssa Zaczek, my genius agency sibling, please give me your description-creating brain. Getting to know you and swapping stories was one of the best things to come out of a stressful year.

Thank you to my wonderful writing community, including Alyssa Colman, Julie Abe, Graci Kim, Karah Sutton, Cassandra Ramos-Gomez, Rochelle Hassan, Ava Wilder, Rachel Greenlaw, Katie LaRae, and many more. Your wisdom, mentorship, and friendship are worth more than a winged pad on a heavy-flow day. A.k.a. you're very appreciated.

The lovely Emma Ewel and Brooke Williams, thank you for reading drafts and giving feedback along the way. So very helpful!

Thank you to my day-ones who went through all the awkward phases with me. You know who you are. I'll be friends with you guys forever since you know too many embarrassing secrets.

My encouraging and supportive parents, Kymberly and Bob. Thank you for always believing in my dreams and for being the best family a girl could ask for. I love you.

And finally, thank you to my partner, Liam. I love you. I love you. I love you.

KARINA EVANS

studied English with a concentration in film at the University of Delaware before going into a career in the entertainment industry. She currently lives in Los Angeles, California. *Grow Up, Tahlia Wilkins!* is her first novel. She invites you to visit her online at karinaevans.com.